"She's falling for you, Deputy."

"Fortunately I'm close by," Mike replied softly. "But what are we doing up at this hour, ladies?" Still holding the child, he dropped his chin to Hannah's hair.

"Bad dream."

"Ah." He snuggled the little girl closer. "I hate those. I never know if I should be mad or sad or scared, so I usually end up in a combination of all three."

Hannah peeked up at him. She blinked twice, as if agreeing. Then she ducked her head again, above his heart, and he didn't want to think about how right this felt. Holding a child. Soothing her fears.

"It's tough," Carly agreed, "but we're learning how to close our eyes and go back to sleep."

"Neat trick. Does that work for you?" Mike asked, teasing.

"I'm so tired when I hit the bed that sleep comes quickly. And I gave up dreaming a long while back."

"I'm sorry." A strong woman like Carly, a person willing to take on four kids, should be the ultimate dreamer.

Multipublished bestselling author **Ruth Logan Herne** loves God, her country, her family, dogs, chocolate and coffee! Married to a very patient man, she lives in an old farmhouse in Upstate New York and thinks possums should leave the cat food alone and snakes should always live outside. There are no exceptions to either rule! Visit Ruth at ruthloganherne.com.

Books by Ruth Logan Herne

Love Inspired

Kendrick Creek

Rebuilding Her Life
The Path Not Taken
A Foster Mother's Promise

Golden Grove

A Hopeful Harvest
Learning to Trust
Finding Her Christmas Family

Shepherd's Crossing

Her Cowboy Reunion
A Cowboy in Shepherd's Crossing
Healing the Cowboy's Heart

Grace Haven

An Unexpected Groom
Her Unexpected Family
Their Surprise Daddy
The Lawman's Yuletide Baby
Her Secret Daughter

Visit the Author Profile page at LoveInspired.com for more titles.

A Foster Mother's Promise

Ruth Logan Herne

LOVE INSPIRED

INSPIRATIONAL ROMANCE

LOVE INSPIRED®
INSPIRATIONAL ROMANCE

Recycling programs
for this product may
not exist in your area.

ISBN-13: 978-1-335-75919-1

A Foster Mother's Promise

Copyright © 2022 by Ruth M. Blodgett

This edition published by arrangement with Harlequin Books S.A.

For questions and comments about the quality of this book, please contact us at CustomerService@Harlequin.com.

Love Inspired
22 Adelaide St. West, 41st Floor
Toronto, Ontario M5H 4E3, Canada
www.LoveInspired.com

Printed in U.S.A.

For I know him, that he will command his children and his household after him, and they shall keep the way of the Lord, to do justice and judgment; that the Lord may bring upon Abraham that which he hath spoken of him.
—*Genesis* 18:19

This one's for Heather and Joel...
It takes a special couple to do what you do
with those sweet babies. God bless you!

Chapter One

Deputy Mike Morris climbed out of his SUV and surveyed his new surroundings, a visual that looked nothing like what he usually encountered in his big-city investigator work back in Nashville.

He was literally tucked between a rock and a hard place as the Smokies rose and rolled around him while the farms and forests surrounding the small town of Kendrick Creek sat in the valley below.

Silence enveloped him.

Mike hated silence.

It left too much time to think. To question. To remember why he'd left the city.

He breathed deep but the quiet of the trees, the rise of the mountains and the roll of the hills oozed tranquility. Too much tranquility, enough to make him rethink his decision. Why was he here? Why had a decorated precinct commander left the job he loved to take a trial position with a rural sheriff's department?

Not to heal his heart. That was a no-go. But a change of scenery and—

Screams and shouts from across the rural road shattered his thoughts.

He raced that way.

He knew the sound of fear when he heard it. Every cop did. He zeroed in on the direction.

Go left.

He withdrew his firearm quietly. Only a fool walked into an unknown situation unprepared, and with over twenty years of law enforcement under his belt, Mike was no one's fool.

The screams came again. Then again.

Figures darted this way and that through the trees behind the house. He didn't have a clean line of sight, so he crept around the edge of a roadside stand of trees.

A woman lay in the grass. Unmoving. Beautiful. Honey-blond hair, tanned skin. Possibly injured or dead.

He didn't hesitate. He rushed to her side to make a quick assessment and saw no visible wounds.

He bent and put two fingers against her neck to check for a pulse.

She screamed.

He may have, too, because she went from being dead to being quite alive and scared to death.

"It's okay." He tucked the firearm back into his waistband and put his hands up. "I'm one of the good guys. I heard the screams and came to help."

"Good guys don't frighten a woman to death in her own front yard." She'd scooched away when she shrieked and stayed crouched in the grass as she eyed him with cool suspicion. "And I promise you, I have lived here for years and there is no one within hearing distance of my screams, and rarely a passerby, so try again."

She was a smart aleck, but then, he *had* come at her with a gun. To save her life, so he still wasn't completely wrong. "I'm Deputy Mike Morris. I'm moving into the house across the street."

Disbelief deepened her features. She stood, refusing his hand out to help, and gazed at him then at the road. "The Littletons aren't coming back?"

"No. It's just me."

Her frown made him wonder if he should have reconsidered his options before accepting the temporary assignment with the sheriff's department here in Cocke County. He would wear the uniform of a deputy for the next three months. The county was going to need a new sheriff. He'd applied and been offered the job, but he'd wanted a test run first. Small-town Tennessee hadn't been on Mike's top ten list, and cops didn't always take to an outsider being brought in. And yet here he was.

Two dark-haired boys raced around the corner of the house.

They slid to a stop upon seeing him.

One gulped.

One scowled.

He wasn't sure which annoyed him more so he went with both. "Who are you and what are you doing to Jo?" demanded the first one. He was the taller of the two.

"You're Jo?" Mike asked the woman. She tucked her shoulder-length hair behind her ears after she'd shrugged the strap of her tank top back into place. "Where's Mom?"

The second boy's scowl deepened. "She *is* our mom. Don't you know anything?"

He knew a sassy kid when he saw one, but he bit his tongue.

"Normally, I'm Carly Bradley," the woman explained. "But today I'm Jo in the play we're doing."

Now it was his turn to frown.

"I'm doing remedial reading with the boys over the summer. Instead of just reading *Little Women*, we were play-acting like the characters did in the book." She must have read his confused expression. "You've never read *Little Women*?"

"The title alone supports your supposition."

"Big, strong men don't read books about families facing harsh times because their men went off to war? Stories of depth and warmth and sacrifice?"

"Everybody in seventh grade reads this," said the first boy, his look of suspicion growing. "Right, Mom?"

"It's on the list in many schools, Isaiah."

"'Cept I shouldn't have to do stupid seventh-grade stuff when I'm only in fifth grade and I won't even like fifth grade at all." The smaller boy—the scowler—drew his brows together again only this time his anger was directed at her. That made Mike want to defend her.

He didn't.

He'd worked with a lot of kids over the years. Sometimes the less said, soonest mended adage worked best. "So y'all are all right?"

"Fine." Bits of grass had clung to her legs. Really nice legs. She brushed the grass flakes off her knees then dusted her hands. "When are you moving in?"

"Right now."

"Ah." She grimaced slightly. "Are you noise-sensitive?"

"Only to people screaming, dogs barking and gunshots. Oh, and radios blaring bad music on a nice afternoon. Good music is fine. Bad music…" He did a firm thumbs-down just as a dog began barking in the house.

Then he heard another noise come through.

Crying.

A baby crying. The sound he heard in his dreams, night after night; a sound he couldn't erase because every time he tried to help the baby, it disappeared. Even in his dreams, he couldn't save his wife and unborn child, and that was a truth he lived with every single awful day.

"Gracie's awake." The bigger boy made the announcement. "Want me to get her?"

"Yes, and hurry before she goes totally ballistic."

The baby's cry pitched higher.

"Too late." The younger boy sounded almost cheerful as the bigger boy dashed off, like a screaming baby was all right.

It wasn't all right, and Mike was pretty sure that no matter what he did, where he went or who he knew, it would never be all right again. He gave her a two-finger salute before he headed back across the road.

He'd wanted something to interrupt the quiet. It surely had. Now he was wondering why he hadn't left well enough alone.

How had a crazy handsome, overreactive, noise-sensitive jerk managed to take over the Littletons' house that quickly? Carly wondered as she hurried inside. Bo Littleton had just gone into assisted living a few weeks ago and Alma had moved to Newport to be closer to him.

Notice you went to "crazy handsome" first. Her brain seemed amused by that. *With that dark hair, gray eyes and square-jawed look you see in the chick-flick romances.*

She shoved that thought aside. There was a reason she avoided feel-good movie channels.

She'd reached for that gold ring once. Epic fail. Mentally she understood that her former husband would have cheated even if she'd been a size zero. Emotionally she'd been on a mental and physical life-change diet ever since and fought the image in her mirror daily. An image she'd learned to ignore because it was never thin enough no matter what she did. Yeah, she avoided those feel-good movies on purpose.

They didn't reflect real life, and she was a real-life kind of gal. Between raising the boys, taking on sweet baby Grace, heading up the youth football fundraising committee and dealing with whatever was happening on Isaiah's football team, her plate was full and about to become fuller.

She would have a fourth child in her care as of tomorrow. Isaac and Isaiah's little sister would arrive under rough circumstances. Tough for the little girl. And probably tough for them, too. Four-year-old Hannah didn't want to be moved, but the system left few choices. Carly hoped and prayed they could smooth things over for the anxious little girl and make her feel at home.

"Hey, sweetie." She feathered kisses over Grace's

rounded cheeks as she took her from Isaiah's arms. "Isaiah, can you let Barney out?"

Barney was the sweet-natured mutt that had come along with the boys eighteen months before.

"Do I have to?"

She bit back a retort. Isaiah's twelve years of life hadn't been easy. Nor had ten-year-old Isaac's. But the more rebellious younger brother was often the more helpful of the two and that irony wasn't lost on her. "Yes."

He started toward the back of the house just as Isaac came through the other way.

The dog took that moment to charge between them.

Barney was midsized, goofy, and it would have broken Isaiah's heart to leave him behind, according to his last foster family. She'd said yes in a moment of weakness she'd been able to regret at leisure. Not because she didn't like dogs. She did like them, but she hadn't had time to do dog-training courses in Newport and the only fellow who'd trained dogs around Kendrick Creek had passed away in the spring.

Isaac fell and banged his arm against the doorframe.

Isaiah scooched by, ignoring his brother's plight as Barney raced for the doggie door. He went through to the yard and started barking up a storm.

Barney rarely barked.

He liked to sit and nap and play like an overgrown puppy.

But not today.

It was as if he'd heard the deputy's words and wanted to push the limits. "Isaac, call Barney back in, please."

Isaac stood, frowning, and gripped his elbow. "He just went out."

"Even so. Call him in."

"He won't come." He shot her a dubious look as he rubbed away the sting. "You know he's got to do stuff before he comes in."

The boy made a good point. He went out the front door, letting it bang behind him. Her fault for not getting a new compressor after Barney sprang the original one a few months back.

Grace was happily feasting on her bottle. Isaiah had gone upstairs. He'd learned that seeking a little quiet time was all right. That was a victory for a boy who'd taken care of his little brother as best he could for years.

Silence reigned in the house as she settled into the rocker to feed the baby.

Not outside.

Not only was Barney barking like a coyote on a rabbit trail, Isaac had turned the garage CD player on and cranked it up, testing his limits. Knowing she was feeding the baby. Knowing what the deputy had said. Acting out intentionally to see if she'd send him away like others had done.

She wouldn't. She was his mother now. He was here to stay. She'd completed the adoption for both boys nearly a year before.

But four kids? Could she handle that?

The music stopped mid-song.

The dog went quiet.

An odd silence reigned until the air was torn by a gunshot. In her front yard.

Her heart seized.

The baby cried out.

Isaiah raced down the stairs. The look of fright on his face broke her heart.

She jumped up, thrust Gracie into Isaiah's arms and raced out the door.

The deputy stood there, tall, strong and stern.

Barney sat on the sidewalk like he normally did, strangely calm, and Isaac was nowhere to be seen.

And on the grass, not far from the deputy's feet, lay a huge raccoon; one of the biggest she'd ever seen.

"You shot him."

"Rabid, I expect. Walking drunk and snarling at the dog."

Her gut churned.

Her chest heaved.

She'd been lamenting about the dog barking, and Isaiah's worries, and hadn't gotten up to see what Barney was actually barking about.

What would have happened if the raccoon had attacked Isaac or Barney? Or Gracie when she brought her out to play in the yard?

Carly broke out in a cold sweat.

Her vision swam.

Her legs went numb.

And the next thing she knew, she was on the grass—not near the raccoon—and in the deputy's arms. For one brief moment it felt like that's where she was meant to be. She struggled to sit then stopped when tiny dots of white light made her head swim. "What happened?"

"You fainted."

She frowned. "Impossible."

His skeptical expression indicated it was, in fact, quite possible.

"I don't faint unless some medical professional comes at me with a monster-sized needle. In which case my blood pressure plummets and I go down. But it's never happened for anything else."

"Sudden shocks can trigger the reflex. I've seen it happen. The kid took off for the woods when he saw me."

"Isaac. He'll come back. He takes a little longer to process things than his brother." She tried to push herself up.

He helped and then stood with her. "There wasn't time to warn you about the shot. The dog was moving closer. Sorry about that."

"You just saved us from a sick wild animal. Don't apologize. Barney's had his shots, but what if it had gotten to Isaac? How awful that would be?"

"Almost as bad as the kid's choice in music," the deputy noted.

He was right. This particular CD didn't have a lot of worthy moments, but supposedly it had belonged to the boys' mother. Isaac didn't play it because he liked the music. He played it because of the familial connection. "I'm sorry. He tests me on everything. And just so you know, he's had lots of practice. He's good at it."

"I've worked with a lot of kids over the years. I get it. Are you okay?"

"Yes." She hated that her voice wavered, because she was okay. Faith had helped her make independence a life skill she took seriously.

Isaiah called from the door right then. "Mom, Gracie smells bad. Real bad."

Diaper change time. "I'm coming, honey."

The deputy noted the raccoon carcass. "Sounds like you're needed. I can dispose of that. Unless your husband would rather do it."

She kept her expression bland. "No husband. Just me and the crew."

"Got a shovel in there?" He motioned to the garage. "If not, I expect there's one across the road."

"On the rack just inside the door."

He moved that way as she headed toward the door. "Got it. Sure you're all right, ma'am?"

"Call me Carly."

A tiny muscle flexed his jaw. The right side. Was it practiced? Or natural? She didn't know and wasn't about to find out, although the slight grimace was downright attractive.

"Carly." He stayed sober but kindly. Southern to the max. The charm aspect only made her more wary. "I'm just checking because you went down fast."

"Thank you, but I'm fine."

Her voice didn't wobble and he seemed to take that as a good sign. "All right." He grabbed the shovel as she climbed the steps.

"And thank you for doing that."

He didn't turn. Didn't wink or tip a finger to his Tennessee Titans ball cap. He gave a quick wave and kept right on moving.

So did she.

Chapter Two

The garage was neat.

Mike appreciated that.

Messy garages unnerved him. Too many places for things to hide. This one was organized. Her car wasn't in the garage. It was parked down the driveway, off to one side, as if leaving room for a second vehicle.

He withdrew the shovel and walked down the driveway toward an open spot. Tree roots would make it impossible to dig in the woods, but he didn't want to tear up her yard, so he picked a spot not far from the woods but off to the side.

The younger boy watched from inside the tree line.

Mike had seen the slivers of blue and white from the kid's T-shirt as he'd moved toward the garage. He pretended ignorance.

He might have traumatized the boy. If he did, better that the kid's mother handle the fallout. Or the kid might be a little punk, plotting trouble from his spot inside the woods' edge.

Not his problem. He knew better than to muddy certain waters for single moms and their kids. He had no business butting in, and it was all he could do to get himself out of bed each morning. Tug on his clothes. Tie his shoes.

His mother had said it would get better.

She'd been right about skinned knees.

She was wrong about heartache.

He dug a hole deeper and wider than probably necessary, but he only wanted to handle the carcass once.

The older boy came his way with a jug of bleach. "Mom said you'd need this." He checked out the deceased and whistled. "That's like the granddaddy of all raccoons around here."

"Yeah?" Mike lowered the raccoon into the hole and started shoveling the dirt back into place. "A lot of raccoons hereabouts?"

"You're not from here, are you?"

He was and he wasn't. He had roots here. Most of the Morris and Kendrick family had moved away when he was a boy, including his parents. Mike shrugged. "I've lived in Nashville a long time."

"Ain't never been." The boy's affect changed quickly. He seemed to rethink his words as if schooled to reconsider. "I mean, I've never been there. But Mom says we'll go someday, though I don't know how now." He frowned at the car. "There's barely room in the car for us. Where are we going to put my little sister?"

"Doesn't she ride in the car seat in the back?" He jutted his chin toward the car.

"Not Gracie. Hannah."

"Another sister?" Mike had no idea what the boy was talking about. He stayed focused on shoveling.

"Yeah. They're bringing her tomorrow. From the foster home she was in," the boy added.

Her kid was in foster care?

Hairs rose along the nape of his neck.

Why had her child been taken from her?

A realm of possibilities darted through his brain. Most of them meant he may have been downright stupid not to do a neighbor check before agreeing to rent this house, because a cop living a stone's throw from a troubled home could spell problems in several ways.

"Is it gone?" The younger boy asked the question from the woods. He sounded scared.

"It's gone," Mike assured him. "I'm going to bleach the shovel now." He didn't make eye contact with the boy. He washed the shovel with bleach by the road's edge, then sat it out in the sun to dry.

"Why'd ya do that?" The younger boy hadn't quite exited the woods, but Mike caught a glimpse of his face. Yup. Scared.

"Bleach kills the virus and the sun dries the bleach."

"Doctors can't fix raccoons when they get sick?"

The kid had a heart. Always a good sign. "Not if it's rabies. And we don't want it spreading to other animals. That's why your mom got shots for your dog."

"Our *new* mom."

"One of many," muttered the older boy. He didn't look argumentative. Just sad and resigned.

Mike had no idea what he meant, but if her kids had been in and out of foster homes, he empathized completely. He'd been surrounded by family and faith all his life. The boy's comment reflected the sorrow of never belonging.

Carly came out of the house then. She was carrying hand wipes and sanitizer. "Use these," she instructed him. Not bossy. But not like he had a choice, either. "And thank you. Thank you for investigating what I should have looked into. You may have saved Barney and Isaac. We're beyond grateful."

"Just doing my job, ma'am." He smiled her way.

She smiled back. A small one. Almost as if she didn't have a lot to smile about.

Him, either. Not his business in any case.

He handed back the wipes and the spritzer bottle then put a single finger to his Titans' cap. "Here's hoping for a quieter evening." The baby started squalling from inside. "I'll let you get back to it. Sounds like you've got your hands full."

"A house of many blessings." She aimed a quiet look at the boys. "God is good, isn't He, boys?"

"Especially good if He figures out a bigger car," the oldest lamented. He wasn't smart-mouthing her. He seemed genuinely concerned about transportation. His brow knit in worry. About the car? Or was there more going on?

"We'll figure it out, Isaiah. We always do."

The boy looked at her. "It was easier when it was just us two." He dropped his gaze to the smaller boy. "A lot easier."

She didn't sigh.

Mike gave her extra credit for that, because four kids in one family wasn't easy under the best circumstances. He knew because he came from a big family with no financial worries, but that didn't make them immune to problems.

This house was nothing like his childhood home, and these kids weren't anything like the five Morris siblings. He had a lawyer brother north of Kendrick Creek, a doctor, a teacher, a cattle ranch owner outside of Nashville, and him, a cop. Odd man out. But successful in his own way.

The younger boy dashed to the house. "I'll get Gracie!" The door banged shut behind him. He emerged quickly with a biggish baby clasped in his arms.

Mike's chest went tight like it always did when he saw a baby these days. Why him? Why Hallie? Why their child? He had a lot of questions with no good answers.

The pudgy girl was strong and healthy. Beautiful. She had a head full of soft black curls. Her gray-green eyes went wide as her brother toted her across the yard. She gazed around as the boy crossed the grass and, when he reached Carly's side, he handed the baby off. "Here you go, Gracie. Here's Mom."

Carly palmed the boy's head in a nice gesture. "Thank you, Isaac. You're such a good big brother." She tipped her gaze up to Mike's. "And thanks again, Deputy."

"Call me Mike. Being neighbors and all."

She accepted that with a polite nod. "Works for me." She began moving toward the house again. When she did, Gracie peeked up over her shoulder and gave Mike one of the cutest baby smiles he'd ever seen. That only made his chest hurt more because his son—his baby—never got the chance to smile.

"If you need help settling in, let us know," called Carly as she neared the door.

"Will do."

That's what he said. But in his head he shouted, No, No, No.

He jogged across the street, weighing what he knew.

Beautiful woman. Troubled kids. Host of problems, seen and unseen. And a healthy, winsome baby.

Not it!

When he was a kid, he and his siblings made declaring "Not it!" an art form. Last one to lay a finger on the side of their nose had to do whatever job Jerusha Morris laid out for them.

That didn't always get them out of the chore, but they had their own code of honor and response time was clutch. Currently his response time was immediate.

He could barely take care of himself these days. He wasn't in any shape to take care of others. The good thing was, he was smart enough to know it.

She'd ignored a dangerous situation because she'd let herself be distracted by worries and the baby's needs. Every time she replayed the timing of the afternoon incident, Carly found herself lacking. Why hadn't she gone to the door and looked outside?

Doubt didn't just niggle her. It swept in because she'd already committed to another little soul, a troubled little girl. A sibling that no one knew existed until last month. But Hannah was quite real and she was arriving tomorrow via a Sevierville County social worker, hence Isaiah's worry.

Isaiah had a heightened awareness that saw too much sometimes. Sensed too much. He was a thoughtful boy who seemed to take the weight of the world onto his shoulders. She understood that because she tended to do the same thing.

When the thought of adopting hard-to-place kids had come to her a few years back, she'd prayed and examined the options. Weighed her choices. And when she'd met with the local social worker to talk about Isaiah and Isaac, she'd read their profiles, their school records and taken the time to get to know them. As a teacher, she made plans. She'd done the same thing for motherhood. Knowing the boys, she'd laid out a plan to help ensure success. Then when the social worker had called about Grace, she'd caved almost instantly. Was that because she understood the pain of separation because she'd been raised in the foster care system?

Yes.

She didn't want that regret for her sons, but was she truly equipped to handle a house with four kids and a full-time job? She was just getting accustomed to three.

The house was quiet.

The boys had gone upstairs to their rooms. Isaiah liked to read at night to relax his brain. Reading helped him sort out the worries of the day.

Isaac attacked bedtime like a cyclone, pushing his favorite toys under his bed. He still didn't believe that his things wouldn't disappear when they were out of his sight, like they had in previous homes.

She'd built trust and love with the boys over the eighteen months they'd been together. Was she eroding that by stretching herself too thin?

She put a glass of cold, sweet tea to her forehead and walked outside to the porch. Gracie was sleeping. She'd been sleeping through the night for months, but teething was messing that up.

How long did that go on? It wasn't like she had practical experience to fall back on.

She had parental leave from school until after the Christmas break, but what then?

Lights glowed across the street. Her new neighbor didn't shut things down at eight o'clock like the Littletons had done. In the quiet of the night she heard his front door squeak open then close.

He had a broad front porch, not the narrower style common to modern houses. Broad enough to house a pair of rockers and a handmade swing, both of which were still there, so maybe the Littletons had sold the house contents and all?

She didn't know.

She'd barely known that Bo's health had deteriorated because she'd been so busy with the baby and the boys.

A new but already familiar figure began walking up her driveway. "You all right?"

She choked back her initial reaction because it had been a long time since anyone had asked. Or cared. "Fine, thanks."

She wasn't fine. She was the opposite of fine, so why did she pretend? Hadn't she learned her lesson when Travis left? Not to bury emotions but deal with them? Especially the bad ones. Fear. Self-doubt. Insecurity.

"That's what most folks say when they're anything but," he told her. He didn't come close. He kept a social distance and she couldn't see his face in the shadows. That didn't matter. She heard the empathy in his voice, as if the rugged deputy understood. "Don't beat yourself up over today."

Of course, that was exactly what she'd been doing. "You must excel at target practice, because you're spot-on right now."

He shrugged. "I do, but I'm pretty good with people, too. It was a scary incident and you didn't realize it was happening."

"I should have checked."

"Were you watching TV?"

She squared her shoulders, trying not to be offended. "No."

"Scrolling on your phone?"

Frustration filled her because who had time to do that with so much on their plate? The kids, the looming football season and fundraiser, a new child soon to arrive? "No. Listen—"

He didn't let her finish. "My point is that you were taking care of your baby. And that things happen. Also, your son was smart enough not to go after the dog or the raccoon. He retreated. The only thing he might want to do differently is to come get you right away."

"That hasn't always been a choice for him, but you're right. I'll go over the steps with him again."

"All's well that ends well," he told her. "My mom says if she beat herself up over everything that could have happened raising five kids, she wouldn't have been around to raise five kids."

"You all survived?" She put the wry note in her tone purposely.

"Every one of us." He took a step back. "But she's got some great stories to tell."

"Hair-raising or poignant?"

"Both." He raised a hand. "I'll head back, but it seemed like you took that on the chin today. And that's a hard notion to rest on."

"How did you know I was out here?"

He waved toward the front lights. "Silhouette."

She kept the outside lights on all night. Every night. She liked a well-lit house and yard. Lights kept the shadows of the past in abeyance. She'd stepped out of the shadows once she was old enough to make her own choices. Chart her own path. She'd been shuffled back and forth from home to home for over twelve years as a child, never the kid people wanted to keep. The sharp blade of a cheating husband struck deep because he hadn't wanted to keep her, either. He'd messed with her self-image, faith and health, confirming that she was better on her own. And that's exactly where she planned to stay. Strong, faithful and independent. If you didn't rely on anyone, no one could let you down.

"You don't see silhouettes as much in the city," he went on. "Too many lights. It's different here."

"I got my teaching degree at the state university in Murfreesboro. Not a big city, but big enough. The lights are different in urban areas."

She couldn't read his expression in the dark, but she heard the solemnity in his voice. "Yeah."

She wasn't sure what to make of that so she settled for a simple thank-you. "Good night, Mike. And thanks again for today."

"Yes, ma'am."

He didn't call her Carly. Was he being cute or maintaining a wise distance?

She didn't know and didn't care, except that being a good neighbor was a thing. Not just with her but her faith.

Love thy neighbor as thyself.

Old true words. And he'd proved worthy today, but she hadn't missed the hint of cautious concern in his earlier tone and expression.

She embraced caution wholeheartedly now. That's why acting out of character to take in Grace and Hannah scared her. Could she do right by all four kids? Or was she still trying to make things better for the bereft little girl she used to be?

She'd do it and she'd do it right, but she wasn't afraid to ask the good Lord's help because she didn't want to trigger herself into an anti-eating frenzy like she'd done before.

She was in charge. She was in control. That's what she'd thought, but she'd learned a lot by adopting the boys. Children's reality wasn't drawn as firmly in the sand, and she'd be the only thing standing between them and a good old Tennessee storm.

That put the onus straight on her. Now her job was to handle it.

Chapter Three

Mike looked over the house room by room the next morning.

The Littletons had left their furniture. He'd agreed to buy what he wanted and have the rest sold by someone local. It was an unusual request, but when the real estate agent explained the elderly couple's sudden change in circumstances, he'd agreed. He could always sell things as needed if he returned to Nashville. He called the number he'd been given once he'd tagged some items.

"Jordan Ash. How can I help you?"

Mike explained his situation and location. "I've never done anything like this," he told her. "I'm at 1432 Klem Trail."

"Alma said she'd left my number with you," the woman replied. "You're renting the Littleton house, correct?"

"Yes."

"Across from my friend Carly."

"Yes." Clearly this was a small-town thing, everyone knowing everyone else.

"I've got time to look at the contents today, if that's convenient for you, Mr...."

"Morris. Deputy Mike Morris. I'm a new member of the sheriff's detail."

"Well, welcome to Kendrick Creek, Deputy." She drawled the words with just enough tang to make this place feel a little more like home. "How's eleven thirty for you?"

"Sounds good."

He ended the call then decided on the plan for the day.

He'd cleaned out the kitchen refrigerator yesterday—an awful job—and decided to tackle the second one in the detached garage today.

That one was less of a challenge. He made appointments for the propane tank to be checked and filled, and when a blonde parked in his driveway at eleven twenty-five, the house didn't smell quite as bad as it had the day before.

"Jordan Ash." She extended her hand quickly. "I know not every cop likes to shake hands, but it's generally how we do things here. Pleasure to meet you."

"Same where I come from," he told her, although she was correct. Some officers backed away from the gesture for various reasons. But Jordan Ash didn't look like she intended to do him bodily harm. "I rolled in yesterday and looked things over this morning. There are several items I want to keep in the house."

"Sometimes buying new or used furniture is easier than moving it from one end of the state to the other," she noted.

It wasn't the ease of purchase that drove him, it was

escaping the memories, but she didn't need to know that. "I'll keep the table and chairs, the stuff in the second bedroom, the living room stuff and the things on the porch." He indicated the swing and the rockers, and the rustic wood chimes. "I've never had a porch and I like this whole thing. It works."

"An invitation to kick back and relax now and again."

"Exactly. And the day-to-day kitchen stuff can stay," he added. "What's the best way to sell the rest? I've got my stuff in a pod waiting to be brought here." He didn't add that renting the pod wasn't a big deal or that he might not even bring his stuff over from Nashville. Not until he'd made a decision. "I'm not in a huge rush, but I want to settle in."

She'd pulled out a notebook and her phone. "Estate sale or auction? This time of year, either works. Then we can have a consignment shop offer a lot price on the balance."

"Like a one-price-takes-all deal?"

"Yes. But let's see what we've got first, all right?"

He led the way up the steps as a car turned into his neighbor's driveway. With their placement on the little-traveled road, any car coming this far was either going to her place or his. Or lost.

Jordan went through the house and the basement. She took pictures. "It's fortunate that Alma didn't waste any time putting the house up for sale, even though it had to be hard for her," she explained as she worked. "Houses that sit too long on the market invite problems. I think we can get a solid price on a lot of this stuff, which will help Alma get established in her new apartment. Are you sure there's nothing else she wants from here?"

He shook his head as a sharp screech of tires interrupted their meeting.

Then the shouting began.

Another game? Play-acting again? Or was this real? He didn't know, but he didn't dare ignore it.

He took off out the door.

Jordan followed him.

He raced down the driveway.

The car that had turned into Carly's driveway earlier was back on the road, headed the other way. Tire marks marred the road's surface. A middle-aged woman was hurrying up the road, calling a name. *Hannah.*

Carly's voice came from the woods, yelling the same name repeatedly.

He went toward her house.

Isaiah was standing in the yard. He was holding the baby. The lost expression on his face hit Mike deep. In twenty-some years being a cop, he'd seen that look of helplessness before, but he always hated to see it on a kid.

"I gotta go look." The younger boy was prowling the edge of the woods. "You know I should, Isaiah."

"Mom said to stay here. That's what I know. We don't need two lost kids to find." The baby squawked in his arms. He tipped her up over his shoulder and patted her back like an expert.

"Who's lost?" Mike asked Isaiah.

"Our sister Hannah." Isaiah's brow creased. "She took off when the social worker was leaving."

"Didn't want to stay?"

Isaiah made a face of confusion. "Who knows? She took off before we could find out anything."

"How old is she?"

"Almost five, Mom said."

Irritation spiked the hairs on his neck.

Didn't they know how old their sister was? Had she been gone that long?

He hit pause on his reaction. He needed to help. Not hinder. "Which way did she go?"

"She ran across the road when the lady was pulling out. But then she ran back again. She was crying, begging the lady to take her with her. Then I couldn't see."

The baby fussed again. So sweet. So small. So innocent.

Injustice flared within him. It took supreme effort to quell it. He saw Jordan hurry into the treed area on his left. Isaac was calling the child's name on his right. Half-heartedly, but he was doing it.

If he were a kindergarten-age kid who didn't want to stay someplace, where would he go?

Away from the voices. As fast and quick as he could. But then he'd be scared because the woodlands were thickly forested and dotted with creeks and ponds. Way too many dangers for a small child.

He went the other way.

He didn't call her name. He stayed absolutely quiet as he looked back from the wooded hillside to triangulate his position with Carly's house and the car.

The car.

Of course.

She wanted to escape, so she'd get back into the car if she could.

He stood still, watching. Waiting. The voices were

moving deeper into the trees on the opposite side of the road.

He stayed quiet. As the voices grew faint, a small figure darted out of the woods less than a hundred feet from him. Small enough that he could have walked within ten feet and never would have seen her. She was in bright pink shorts and a sparkly unicorn shirt. Twin golden-brown braids hung down her back. They bounced when she made a beeline for the car. He wasn't even sure she was strong enough to get the car door open, but she did. Then she scrambled into the back seat, pulled it shut softly and disappeared from view.

He didn't have his neighbor's phone number so he texted Jordan. I've got her. She's in the car on the road. I'll keep an eye out.

The woods went quiet as the women shared the information, most likely.

Then he spotted Carly coming through the woods.

He thought she'd be scared.

He thought wrong.

Determined, yes.

Scared, no.

She waved a thumbs-up to where Isaiah was standing, then crossed the narrow grove of trees.

Mike pointed to the car.

She nodded. Then motioned him closer.

She didn't want the girl escaping again. Neither did he. He closed in from his side.

He heard the other two women coming through the brush. He ignored them and kept his eyes on Carly.

Kids were taken away from parents for a variety of reasons, but they had to be good reasons.

Hurting a child or being mean or abusive to one wasn't something a cop liked to see, but after years of not being able to have a child, he knew he was more vulnerable to emotions in bad situations.

You don't know why the girl was taken away. No snap judgments allowed. You know better.

The mental warning was correct. Assumptions rarely worked in family situations, and he was the new kid on the block.

He stood off to the side. Close enough to block the child's escape, but not so close as to spook her.

Carly opened the car door.

The door on his side didn't fling open. The girl was too small for that, but she was giving it her best shot. He moved closer, blocking her way, and when she raised those big blue eyes to him, his heart didn't just go soft.

It melted.

She leapt for him when the door gave way, as if he were a saving grace.

She buried her face into his neck and shoulder, seeking sanctuary from whatever life had thrown her way.

So small. So precious. So innocent.

The older woman was heading their way. She was huffing and puffing some, but she marched down that road at a quick clip. "You'll need the locks set when she's not right with you, Ms. Bradley. Strong ones set high enough she can't reach. These woods aren't any place for a youngster, you mark my words, and this one doesn't take friendly to rules. Anyone's rules."

Carly didn't answer. She rounded the vehicle quietly. Then she reached for the girl.

The girl clung tighter to Mike. And when she grabbed

harder, she didn't just grab his well-washed gray T-shirt. She grabbed his heart. He jutted his chin toward the door. "Okay if I bring her in for you?"

The child shuddered.

Carly offered a resigned nod.

He crossed the front yard as Jordan Ash emerged from the woods. She looked at the child, then at Carly, but remained quiet.

Carly moved ahead and opened the front door as the social worker's car started up. The engine noise diminished as the car headed for the bigger road below.

The child stared in the direction of the sound and the lost look on her little face hit him crosswise again.

He stepped into the house.

Carly and Isaiah followed. Jordan stayed outside with the younger boy.

The house was lived-in but tidy. The two rooms he could see bore none of the typical bad environment benchmarks. No broken doors, damaged wallboard, crooked cupboards.

This house was nice. Fairly neat and absolutely solid.

The girl still clung to him.

He turned and met Carly's gaze. Then he lifted a brow in question because he wasn't sure what to do next. He hadn't been called to help, so he settled into a sturdy recliner.

Carly came closer.

The baby in Isaiah's arms began crying. It wasn't a loud cry, but it grew more insistent as the seconds stretched on.

"There are peaches and cereal on the counter, Isaiah."

"Okay."

He didn't argue. Resigned, he moved toward the kitchen area and tucked the baby into a high chair. He strapped her in like a pro then proceeded to feed her the contents of the dish on the counter.

Carly knelt on the floor, alongside his feet. She reached out a hand to the little girl's back. "Hannah."

The girl tucked her chin. Tears trickled down her peaches-and-cream-toned cheeks. Cheeks that were different than Gracie's, but there was a similarity, too.

Her tears soaked into the weave of his shirt.

"Are you hungry, Hannah?" Carly soothed with her soft voice and gentle touch. "Mrs. Wilkins said you didn't eat this morning."

No answer.

"How about some apple juice?" Carly held up a juice box. She applied the little straw to the box and held it out.

Hannah only dug her face deeper into Mike's neck.

He reached out a hand and raised a brow at the juice.

Carly handed it to him.

"Hey, Miss Hannah." He whispered the words in a gentle tone and, for some reason, the girl peeked up at him from her spot against his chest. "Juice sounds mighty good 'bout now, doesn't it, darlin'?"

She gazed at him. Then she reached up and patted his cheek, as if checking to see if he was real. She stared at him.

He looked back.

Then he handed her the juice box. She studied it, then him, and when she finally sipped from the tiny straw, he felt like he'd just scored a touchdown. She sipped long and hard, not stopping for air. When the juice was gone, she handed him the little box and reburied her head in his neck.

Jordan came in the front door. She sized up the situation then addressed him. "I can see you're busy, Mike, so if next weekend sounds good, we'll get this sale going. I'll send Alma the contract, and I'll be sure to exclude the things you're keeping. I'll leave the pricing of that to you and Alma, all right?"

"I appreciate it."

"I'll call you to set up a time when I can come in and tag everything."

"Sounds good."

She nodded, then turned to Carly. "Carly, do you need anything? I know you've got your hands full. Do you want me to take over the fundraiser? Buy you some time?"

"That is tempting, but no. Although I could use your help on it," Carly replied. "We've got nearly five weeks. Things should be settled down by then."

Carly sounded confident but Jordan still looked skeptical.

"Call me anytime, okay? I can be here in minutes if you need a hand."

"You know I will."

Jordan turned back his way. He mouthed *Thank you.* She smiled in return.

"Don't mention it. That little one seems mighty tucked in right now, and I'm not one to disturb a quiet child. Doin' so would only make me out to be the foolish one."

Jordan slipped out. She caught the door and didn't let it slam, like she knew it would. A regular visitor, then.

Ten minutes later, the little girl's breathing softened. It evened out. He couldn't see her face, but when Carly came alongside, she bent over.

Soap and sunshine.

She smelled like the softness of soap and the sweetness of fresh Tennessee air on a non-humid day. "Sound asleep," she whispered. "I've got a bed ready for her here on the first floor, near me. She'll be sharing a room with Grace."

He stood, barely daring to breathe, and when she stayed asleep, he considered it a minor victory. He followed Carly into one of two bedrooms at the back of the house, and the first thing he checked for was window locks.

When he spotted them, he breathed easier. They were high enough that Miss Hannah wouldn't be able to access them. He went to set her down on the bed.

She stirred, so he bent with her, letting her nestle into the pink-and-white-striped sheets and the bright pink pillowcase with another smiling unicorn.

The unicorn's happiness annoyed him.

Of course it was happy. It was fictional. It didn't exist in the real world of rough choices and hard days. But he couldn't deny that the unicorn's whimsical face was engaging for a kid.

The girl stirred, started sucking her thumb and settled in.

He tiptoed out of the room with Carly and when they got to the living room, he let out the sigh he'd been holding for way too long. "What's the plan for when she wakes up?"

Carly met his gaze. "Keep her safe until she gets used to being here? New places can be hard on kids."

"She's never been here before? Or she was too young to remember?"

She stared at him and he could tell when realization took hold. Because her eyes narrowed. "She's never been here before because we didn't know she existed until recently."

Now it was his turn to frown. "I don't get it."

"I see that." She kept her voice soft. Really soft. Then she motioned outside. "I adopted the boys eighteen months ago. I was in the foster system when I was a kid. I was handed around from house to house. When my marriage fell apart and I knew there were lots of kids needing good homes, I decided to adopt Isaac and Isaiah. I've always wanted to be a mother and my prospects had thinned by then. When you don't have good parents, being a great mom or dad can become your number-one childhood wish. At least, that's how it was for me," she admitted.

"I'm a teacher," she continued. "I'm great with kids, and I had no trouble seeing myself handling two boys who needed faith, hope, love and football. But…" She paused and her voice deepened slightly. "Then the social services department called to say that their mom had Grace and was relinquishing her. How could I say no to taking their baby sister? I took family leave from school until January, and it seemed like it would all work out. Then we found out about Hannah two weeks ago. She was in another county and never got cross-referenced with her brothers, so when the relationship was discovered, I got another phone call. And here I am with four kids."

Not her kids.

Not taken from her for any reason. She'd taken them in to give them a home.

He'd assumed the worst and Carly was giving these kids the best opportunity she could. He shifted his gaze from the kids outside to Carly.

Her eyes met his, and there it was again. The connection. Unexpected yet quite real. It was a nice surprise because he hadn't felt that way in a long time.

Her compassion called to him. And she was beautiful in a way that younger women couldn't be. She'd lived her life successfully despite dealing with some hard knocks. That called to the fixer in him. The protector. But it was a call he wouldn't be answering. No way. No how.

He'd buried his wife and baby son, two lives that shouldn't have been lost if the doctors had talked to one another. Or if they had used the same electronic system. Or if his wife—his beloved Hallie—had told her obstetrician what the fertility specialist knew. That she'd had an eating disorder that had caused cardiac problems several years ago.

Somehow that information never got relayed, and when her heart gave out weeks before the baby was due, she was gone. The baby was gone. And Mike had been left with nothing but a gaping hole where a heart and soul used to reside.

Carly would need help, most likely. At least from time to time, but that's what Jordan and her other friends were for. Right? Because he'd made a decision when they'd lowered that casket into the ground. He'd given his heart once and it had nearly killed him.

He'd vowed never to risk it again.

He'd be a good neighbor. And maybe a nice role model for those boys. But that's where it would end. Because it didn't matter how much help she'd need. It simply wasn't his to give.

Chapter Four

Getting into the car for football practice or games used to take ten minutes. Today the process had taken an hour by the time she'd sweet-talked Hannah into brushing her hair and washing her lovable little face. They'd managed the clean face. Cute hair wasn't a battle Carly had had time to wage.

She got the boys to practice in the nick of time. When the coach made you run a lap for every minute you're late, punctuality took on major importance.

Now she had two hours with Grace and Hannah. She didn't dare let Hannah run and play so close to the wooded area while she amused Grace. Should she take them back home? Take a walk?

Even the thought of a walk in an unrestricted environment seemed foolish after Hannah's escape attempt the day before. She'd ordered a double stroller, but it wouldn't arrive for forty-eight hours. She was contemplating her options when Jordan called. She swiped the screen quickly. "Hey, Jordan."

"What are you up to?"

She kept her voice low. "Trying to decide how to safely navigate the next two hours in an uncontrolled environment. How about you?"

Jordan was totally sympathetic. "I hear you. I've got the Trembeth girls for a few days. I was thinking it might be fun for them to meet Hannah. Izzie's younger than Hannah, but you know that Gracie will think little Beth is one step up from a hot, buttered biscuit."

"I think that's a great idea."

"The playground behind the church?" suggested Jordan. "It has clear perimeters for our little runner."

She made a valid point. Carly agreed. "Ten minutes. I'll bring crackers."

"And I have juice boxes."

"It's a plan."

They met at the playground. A few other families were there, including a couple of Tennessee Junior Volunteer Football parents, but the big, open playground was in the middle of a grassy field behind the church. There was no thick forestland to aid and abet Hannah's escape.

Jordan pulled into the parking lot just after Carly. "Here we are."

Izzie was nearly four. She independently undid her car seat straps and hurried through the open car door. Then she dashed for the raspberry-and-lime-green-colored playground. The orphaned child loved her independence.

At age two, Beth was more laid-back. The sisters had been living with their great-grandparents when the fire swept through Kendrick Creek last December. For seven months, people had taken turns caring for the girls to keep them close to home. As long as the girls were well cared for, the county wouldn't remove guardianship from Ed and Hassie Trembeth despite their age and growing health problems. But the helping hands were a stopgap. Not a long-term solution.

"Would you have pictured this a year ago?" whispered Jordan as Hannah pretty much ignored Izzie's attempts at friendliness.

Carly shook her head. "Nope. The boys and I would go home to a fairly quiet house, with a noisy dog who loves us, and call it a day." Carly shared a *what happened?* look with Jordan.

Jordan laughed, set Beth onto the wood-chipped playground and watched her run straight to Grace's side in the stroller. "And yet, here we are. Blessed. And a little beat-up." She motioned to a series of scratches on Carly's arm. "Hannah?"

"No, she's not one bit aggressive," said Carly. "Wild roses while hunting for her yesterday. Or wild berries. The woods are thick with canes. I'm sending the boys berry picking tomorrow so we can make jam."

"We're becoming positively domestic." Jordan nudged Carly with her elbow and grinned. "How's your new neighbor doing?"

"Don't know." Carly kept her gaze forward.

"Right."

She heard the skepticism in Jordan's voice and decided to cut that speculation off at the pass. "He seems nice. And distant. Which makes him perfect," Carly replied. "It's good to have nice neighbors. And that's all that matters."

"Well, I'm going out on a limb here and saying

there's a whole lot more that matters, but you do you."
Jordan rolled her eyes. "He's nice, caring, single and
smokin' hot. Yes—" she angled a sideways glance at
Carly "—I noticed."

Jordan had been after her to step out of her quiet,
lonely existence prior to the boys' arrival. A part of
Carly understood that Jordan wasn't wrong, but it wasn't
right, either.

"At some point, the good Lord's going to put someone in your path, Carly, and you're going to have no
choice in the matter."

Carly burst out laughing and pointed to Hannah and
Grace. "Already did. And if I can make this work without all of us needing extensive therapy, that's enough
for the moment. It's God's timing that got me into this
and—"

She got cut off by the elongated screech of the volunteer fire department whistle. Loud and piercing, the
alarm screamed its call twice. An ambulance call, then.
No fire.

Hannah put her hands to her ears and shrieked.

Gracie burst into tears and that made Beth cry, because no one cried alone in little Beth's presence.

And then, in almost synchronized fashion, text message alarms began going off across the playground.
Including Carly's. Coach is dead. Mom, come quick!

Coach Wynn, the Junior Volunteers' head coach?
The one who'd kept the football program alive this year
when so many volunteers had had to step aside to fix
homes and barns and businesses?

Carly's heart sank. An icy chill raced down her spine.

"Jordan, something's happened to Coach Wynn. Isaiah just texted me."

"Go." Jordan motioned to Carly's car. "I'll watch the girls here."

"But Hannah—"

"We'll be fine. I'll call for reinforcements."

She'd try, but most parents their age had sons playing football or daughters at cheer practice right now, the two most popular sports programs in this part of the county.

"I've got this," Jordan insisted. "Go."

Carly raced for the car. The field was only about four minutes up the road, not far from the high school.

She pulled off to the side as several sheriff's deputies raced by her, lights flashing and sirens blaring.

Adrenaline surged through her.

Coach Wynn was beloved in this town. He loved to say that he was the "winningest" coach in Kendrick Creek history, and that wasn't a play on his name. It was the rock-solid truth, and his tough-love attitude had turned a lot of troubled boys into responsible, law-abiding citizens. The whole town turned out annually to raise money for the football and cheer programs so that any kid could play, regardless of income.

Isaiah and Isaac loved him. They respected him. And that made what Isaiah had recently shared with her about kids cheating less disturbing, because Coach Wynn didn't break rules. He strategized. If some of the kids were deliberately messing up, he'd take care of it.

Right now she was worried about her boys. What more should they have to deal with? The fire, its aftermath, watching the town change before them, two unexpected little sisters, a rabid raccoon and now—

The ambulance and rescue vehicles raced in from the north. A deputy's SUV was parked out on the field and a familiar form was stretched out, on the ground, working on Coach.

She pulled off into the grassy parking area, hopped out of the car and raced for the sidelines. Two of the assistant coaches seemed overwhelmed. They were new because so many people were still working to rebuild or recover from the fire. Two others were counseling the boys while sneaking peeks over their shoulders to see what was happening. And all the while Mike Morris and a pair of EMTs worked on what seemed to be a lifeless body.

God, please. Please. Please.

She paused the silent prayer and faced the huddling boys. Isaiah had his arm around Isaac, and the crowd of over five dozen boys looked scared, lost and dreadfully alone.

Almost in unison the boys looked her way. When they did, she began to pray.

"Dear God, dear Father in heaven, we ask your peace and grace and healing on Coach. We love him, Lord, we love his heart, his spirit, his drive, his lessons. Maybe we don't love practice all the time, or running laps, but we love Coach Wynn and we just humbly ask you to heal him. Leave him with us. Give us more seasons. Because we need him, Lord. We need him. Amen."

A chorus of amens followed suit.

She opened her arms and hugged any kid that needed it as other parents arrived. Some cried, but most stayed stoic because that was one of coach's lessons. *Stand strong. Chin up. Shoulders square. Chest out. Never let 'em see you sweat.*

Tonight the sweat of practice, gear, heat and emotion mixed with tears, but once Coach had been loaded onto a gurney, Isaiah moved forward and began a slow clap.

The slow clap was what they did when they honored an injured player, increasing the speed and velocity to high as the player came off the field.

It wasn't just the teams, either. Every parent, deputy, first responder and bystander joined in, hoping Coach heard the send-off they were giving him as Mike Morris came their way.

He looked grim.

He came to a stop before them, standing straight and tall, a force to be reckoned with. As he faced the group he kept his gaze on the boys and the other coaches. "Two things. Coach is in a bad way, but we haven't lost him yet. A chopper is landing at the high school to take him to Knoxville. They'll keep us posted from there."

"We prayed for him, sheriff." It was one of the younger boys, and his earnest voice made Carly's throat go tight. "Isaac's mom said a prayer and we all felt it. God won't let him die, will he?"

Mike went silent. But then he answered the boy. "I don't know. But I'm glad y'all prayed together. That's what teams do."

"You said there were two things," noted one of the coaches. "What was the other?"

Mike hesitated. He grimaced slightly, then lifted his chin. "He asked me to step in and take his place. I told him I'd consider it an honor."

Two of the coaches looked happy about this unex-

pected reprieve because being a head coach wasn't a job
for the faint of heart. Everything landed at your feet and
folks that loved winning hated losing in equal fashion.

"Why you?" It was Brice Masterson, the Under-
13 offensive coach asking, and Carly knew why. He'd
been angling for Coach's job for several years, and this
would be a great time to grab the power. He had boys
on both teams, just like her, separated because of the
two-year age difference. "Who are you?" Brice asked.
He frowned slightly as if he should know.

"Mike Morris. *Deputy* Morris. I just moved to town."

"Mike Morris the Tennessee running back while
Manning played?" A younger coach's eyes went wide.
"Weren't you drafted to the NFL your senior year?"

The boys' visible appreciation of the uniformed deputy grew as the young coach spoke.

"Until your injury," noted Jim Lightfoot. Jim had
been Coach Wynn's defensive coordinator for nearly
two decades and he seemed happy to know that coaching thirty-plus boys wasn't going to fall on his shoulders. "I hate when that happens."

Mike shrugged. "It was a long time ago, but Coach
knew me. He's friends with my older brother. You guys
okay if I step in?"

Three nodded instantly.

Not Brice Masterson. "Old experience is still old."

Mike leveled a look his way. Not scolding. But not
matter-of-fact, either. He met Masterson's gaze. "I've
coached fourteen seasons of youth football in Nashville. A winning record, but more importantly it gave
a lot of kids a chance to be someone on the field. Kids
who didn't feel like much when they were off the field."

"You get my vote." Jim Lightfoot was clearly unimpressed by Masterson's attitude. "Good to have you on board. Will you be able to figure out your work schedule?"

"I'll talk to the sheriff tonight."

Masterson still looked skeptical. "Sheriff Byrne doesn't like to be disturbed at home."

"No one does. But my guess is he already knows what happened to Coach and is praying for him."

"You'll be coaching my team." It was Isaiah who spoke up. He indicated the bigger boys. "And if some of the guys come over to my house, can you give us pointers?"

"You like extra practice?" asked Mike.

"With you?" asked one of Isaiah's teammates. "Yeah!" He fist-pumped the air. "I'll do whatever you want, Coach!"

Brice Masterson swallowed hard.

Then he faced the other coaches. "Should we call it for tonight? Get back together tomorrow night, as scheduled?"

The coaches seemed uncertain, and it was Isaiah who spoke up again. "Is that what Coach woulda wanted?"

The boys all knew the answer to that.

"I say we stay," said a littler fellow, one of Isaac's teammates. "Coach would want us to do our best."

The young assistant coach agreed. "Out of the mouths of babes," he told his cohorts. "B Team, with me. Up field! And don't move slow," he warned as he began to backpedal.

"We can stay," agreed Brice. "Finish up practice."

He was trying to put on a good face, but Carly didn't miss the struggle in his expression.

"I'll see you guys tomorrow. Thanks, Coach Masterson." Mike addressed Brice Masterson directly.

Masterson stayed silent. He dipped his chin slightly, but the lack of reply wasn't lost on anyone there. A decent-sized crowd had gathered and the parents began to ply Mike with questions.

He raised his hands and they got quiet.

"A quick heads-up before I get back to work. I have the certification and credentials to do this. Coach actually reached out to me when my brother told him I would be working here. He offered me a chance to work with him and the team. I wasn't ready to commit when he called me," he admitted, "but circumstances have changed."

The sound of chopper blades rising to the north punctuated his remarks.

"But I'm happy to stand in and I'm hoping Coach Wynn is going to do just fine."

"We'll be praying for him," said one mother. Others agreed, nodding.

"Sure will."

"Us, too, Coach!"

He looked down for a moment and Carly saw what no one else did: a look of regret so raw that she wasn't sure how he'd hide it.

And then he did.

He caught her watching him. His eyes stayed on her for two beats longer than necessary before he faced the group again. "All appreciated, folks. I've got to get back to Newport."

"Of course, Deputy. Thank you. You did well." Doc Mary, a mountain woman who had served as Kendrick Creek's doctor for over forty years, smiled at him. "It's good you were here. Your quick intervention might have saved his life."

Carly fell into step beside him as he strode back to his cruiser. "You've just won the hearts of a lot of people in this town. When Doc Mary gives her approval, folks listen. She's saved a lot of lives here, and helped a lot of others."

"A cornerstone."

Carly made a face of regret. "A cornerstone whose battle with cancer is going to end soon."

When they got to his SUV, she looked up at him. The sun hit her square in the face and he moved to block its rays. The cool shade of his shadow felt good. So good.

Kind and strong. She found that attractive but knew her limitations. There was enough on her plate right now.

"The boys love football?" He posed it as a question.

She nodded. "They'd played pickup games and flag football with their foster family, but I got them involved with Coach as soon as I brought them here. They've never had a strong father figure in their lives. They did have nice foster families," she amended, "but no place they really belonged, you know? I wanted to make sure they integrated into the community right away."

"And sports help with that."

"Yeah." She smiled up at him. "I played baseball in high school. Not softball," she explained, and when he grinned, she knew she'd made her point. "I'll never understand the sense of having women with smaller hands play with a bigger, harder-to-throw ball. Ridiculous. Anyway, I was the varsity third baseman. Because of that, I felt like somebody in a town where I had nobody of my own. That meant a lot to me. Those coaches gave me a chance to be something special. Like Coach Wynn has done for years. It means a lot to kids who don't have strong support systems." She stepped back. "Have a good night, Mike. And no worries." She indicated the busy fields with a glance. "You'll have a whole lot of people backing you up."

You made a commitment on that football field tonight. Now you have to keep it.

It wasn't the thought of the game that sucker punched Mike. He loved football.

It was the commitment.

The air in the SUV cruiser thickened as if challenging his right to breathe.

He opened the window. Took a breath. A deep one. Calmed his heart with the slow, deep breaths he'd learned from an online video because he hadn't wanted to waste a therapist's time. Or his. He'd handle this his way.

His brain scoffed at that.

Mike ignored the mental chastisement as he cruised a mountain road, familiarizing himself with the area.

The night breeze bathed him. It felt different, in a good way. To his right and left, mountain curves stretched like the emptiness within him.

Then he remembered Carly's smile. Frank and engaging. And how she'd played hardball because she was that good. He almost smiled because thinking of that made the evening's events less traumatic. He gripped the steering wheel tighter.

He'd just committed to staying around for several months. The season would take them through October. That was a month longer than he'd agreed to work with the county sheriff, but money wasn't the problem. He could afford to take a month off, if needed.

It was the commitment.

Kids counting on him. Parents, too. He'd stopped coaching when Hallie died. He'd stopped doing everything, he admitted to himself as he turned off the Foothills Parkway toward the new business district.

The renovated town center shone with fresh paint and three new buildings. American flags lined the attractive Main Street–styled area. It wasn't called Main Street, and the business district wasn't a village, or even a town, technically, but it had the feeling of a small town and that seemed right.

His phone rang. His older brother Kevin's name flashed in the display. He hit the receive button on the SUV's console to answer. "Hey, what's up?"

"Just checking in to see how it's going. Mom made me. Said she didn't want to be intrusive, but if I called, it was like brotherly love or something obviously untrue like that."

That sounded like Mom, pushing the Morris boys to dig for information. "You can put her mind at ease. Tell her I'm fine."

"Are you?"

"Yep."

"I can still take you, Mike. With one hand tied behind my back. Don't lie to me."

Kevin couldn't take anyone. He was a string bean of a doctor in a lucrative practice outside Nashville. But he was also one of the smartest and kindest people on the planet, so Mike would probably let him win. Just because. "Hanging in. Suddenly committed to a project and didn't want to be. So I have to wrap my head around that." He explained to Kevin what happened.

His brother whistled softly. "That is a commitment. And good for you. How's the new house?"

"In the middle of nowhere," Mike confessed. "So that's weird."

"I bet. You have to drive a fair piece to get to the middle of nowhere around Nashville now. Too quiet, Mike?" Kevin didn't hide the note of concern.

"Not as quiet as I thought at first. I've got noisy neighbors. Well, noisy kids, anyhow, and two of them play football."

"Could be a nice connection."

Kevin had been trying to get him moving in a new direction for months. His encouragement was part of the reason Mike had applied for the sheriff's position in Kendrick Creek. "It's football, Kev. Nothing more."

"There's a lot of potential therapy in throwing a pigskin around," Kevin argued.

There was truth in that.

Just then a police call came through. "Gotta go."

"Talk to you soon. I love you, kid."

Mike's cheek twitched slightly. He was forty-eight years old. Kevin had just turned fifty, and still called him "kid." Probably always would. "Love you, too."

Mike headed to the call: a neighbor dispute in a more rural area of Kendrick Creek.

Upon arrival, he heard the neighbors arguing over a cat using a flower garden as a litter box.

A farm cat, he knew, was useless if kept inside, and the newer neighbor had chosen to build his upscale house fairly close to the property line, which meant the prowling cat was pretty much a given. He listened to them, spoke some common sense and left, hoping for the best.

He finished his shift on a quiet note and when he pulled into his driveway shortly before midnight, he climbed out of his SUV, hoping he was too tired to think and tired enough to fall sleep.

Music floated his way.

He couldn't tell the song, but the plaintive notes rose and fell in quiet rhythm, almost like—

A lullaby.

His heart clenched for the third time that night. He was pretty sure that couldn't be a good thing, yet he followed the music across the street.

Carly was on her small porch. It wasn't wide like his, and held no porch swing, but she was nestled into the single rocker, crooning to a blanket-wrapped figure.

Gracie.

She put a finger to her lips as he drew closer.

He nodded, gave a thumbs-up to show he understood and began walking backward toward his place.

A head popped up.

Hannah. Not Gracie. She spotted him in the lighted driveway and half dove out of Carly's arms. She raced his way and leapt into his arms, claiming his heart all over again.

She didn't talk.

She clung. She clung so tight to his neck that he had to reach up and loosen her grip. "I've got you, pretty girl. I've got you."

He walked to the porch, expecting wrath or at least anger that he'd disturbed Carly.

He saw neither in her expression. "She's falling for you, Deputy."

"What are we doing up at this hour, ladies?" he asked softly. Still holding the child, he leaned against the squared support and dropped his chin to Hannah's hair.

"Bad dream."

"Ah." He snuggled the little girl closer. "I hate those. I never know if I should be mad or sad or scared, so I usually end up in a combination of all three."

Hannah peeked up at him. She blinked twice, as if agreeing. Then she ducked her head again, above his heart and below his ear, and he didn't want to think about how right this felt. Holding a child. Soothing her fears.

"It's tough," Carly agreed, "but we're learning how to close our eyes, roll over and go back to sleep."

"Neat trick. Does that work for you?" Mike asked, teasing, but he wasn't quite prepared for her answer.

"I'm so tired when I hit the bed that sleep comes quickly. And I gave up dreaming a long while back."

The double entendre struck him. "I'm sorry." A strong woman like Carly, a person willing to take on four kids, should be the ultimate dreamer.

"Maybe too tired to dream isn't a bad thing," she whispered. For a moment, he thought she'd read his mind. "What brought you over?"

"The song."

"I'm sorry. I didn't realize it was that loud."

He shook his head as he rocked Hannah. "Don't be. It was pretty. It called to me."

"Like Odysseus and the Sirens?"

He laughed softly. "Should I put wax in my ears and lash myself to the porch railings?"

Her smile deepened, but the smile didn't ease the tired look. "We are a noisy crew. Since you're here, I wanted to thank you again for what you did tonight. It was amazing. And the volunteer fire department sent out word that Coach Wynn is in critical but stable condition. He wouldn't have had that chance without you."

"Just doing my job."

She scolded him with a look. "Do you always have this much trouble accepting compliments?"

He cringed. "I'm afraid so."

"Well…you need to get over that," she said. She stood and stretched. Then yawned. "I'm done in. Let's get her into bed. I'll sleep with her, if it helps."

The lulled sound of Hannah's breathing indicated that might not be necessary. "I think she's out."

"Until we open the creaky door. My fault because I ran out of WD-40."

"I've got some. I'll spray the hinges tomorrow."

"You don't—"

He put a finger to his lips and motioned to the door. She opened it.

He hoped the dog would stay asleep, and when he did, Mike considered that a victory. He tiptoed into the girls' room, gently placed Hannah down onto the striped sheets and unicorn pillowcase.

He wanted to kiss her good-night. But that would be weird coming from him, wouldn't it?

He straightened and eased from the room.

Carly was waiting in the living room. "All quiet on the Western Front?"

"Do you feel like you're revisiting junior high literature regularly?" he asked. He remembered reading a lot of books in junior high. Books that made him think. Pray. Wonder.

"Working on schoolwork with the boys is the best refresher course ever." She grinned "Thanks for coming over, Mike. It was nice."

"It felt nice."

His words made her smile.

Then he smiled and didn't want to stop smiling. It felt good. He'd have probably stayed right there, smiling at her, until she cleared her throat.

He took a step toward the door. "I'm out. Get a good night's sleep, Carly."

"I look that bad, huh?" She rolled her eyes. "It's been a long day."

"Not bad. Just deserving of rest."

Her eyes went wide. Her chin trembled. He realized she probably didn't get a whole lot of emotional support with this motherhood business.

That support wasn't his to give, but if he could be a good neighbor, that wasn't a bad thing. And just maybe it would be good for both of them.

Chapter Five

Mike stopped over at Carly's house late afternoon the next day. He rapped softly on the screen door in case anyone was sleeping.

The dog barked and raced to greet him. His shaggy tail wagged a welcome, but no one else seemed to notice he was there.

He knocked again.

The dog looked around, similarly puzzled by the fact that there were no people.

Her car was there. Unless they'd gone off with someone else?

But no one would leave their front door open with just the screen door closed if they'd left. Would they?

They might if they have four kids to run around everywhere they go. Or if there's an emergency.

That thought got his attention. He tried the door.

Unlocked.

That only deepened his frown, but that was his Nashville experience talking. Mike was pretty sure half the folks in Cocke County didn't bother locking anything.

He started down the porch steps when a fairly loud screech came from the woods. Not a people screech. A machine screech. He went that way and, when he got about forty feet into the woods, he stopped and whistled softly when he spotted Carly in a tree. She was wearing jeans, despite the heat, and a short-sleeved shirt. Bark against skin was a rough combination. "You're trying to build a treehouse?"

Carly scoffed from her perch in the tree. "No trying about it, sir. I'm doing."

Her words made him grin. He tried not to notice how cute she looked up there with a tool belt clasped around her waist. Isaiah and Isaac were holding boards in place while Hannah watched. She seemed fascinated by the sight of Carly in the tree and she wasn't trying to run away.

Carly noted the direction of his gaze. "Who knew that power tools and a mom in a tree could hold the attention of a four-year-old?"

"I'm pretty impressed myself. Where'd you learn to build?"

"Self-taught." She then directed her attention to the preteen boys. "Guys, we've got the anchor bolts set, so we have to call it a day. Let's grab some sandwiches and get you to practice. If you two feed yourselves, I'll wrap up the tools."

"You sure?" asked Isaiah. His glance took in the array at the base of the tree. "I don't mind helping, Mom."

"I'll help her get everything back to the house," offered Mike. "Is Gracie sleeping?"

Carly pointed to the monitor on her tool belt. "Yes. I heard the dog bark when you came, but she'd only been down for half an hour, so it didn't wake her. Her teeth are bothering her at night, so she's not sleeping like she used to."

"That makes her nap more welcome, I expect," he said as she handed the power tools down. He was determined not to notice the cute ponytail or how well those jeans fit as she swung down from the branch and landed lightly at his feet.

"From her perspective, yes."

"No naps for moms," he noted as he carried the battery-powered drill and nail gun.

"Plenty of time for rest in the grave," she answered. When he sent her a dubious look, she laughed. "Ben Franklin. And others."

"The benefits of a teaching career arise again."

"Franklin is one of my faves," she told him. "I love the practicality of his advice. Truly inspiring." She undid the tool belt as she walked and shifted it to her left hand. "I planned to take the boys up to Independence Park. Now we'll do it when the girls are older. Or maybe have someone watch the girls for a few days and give the boys a quick history trip up north. Have you ever been there?"

Mike shook his head. "Never been to Philly. We tended to stay in the South for vacations. And then there was football and work, but I never got a chance to play against a Philly team. You vacationed there?"

"I went to school there. Penn."

The University of Pennsylvania was an Ivy League school. "So...you're smart."

He thought he saw a flash of regret in her face as they emerged from the woods. "Smart enough to know I needed a solid education and there was too much temptation down here for me to stay focused. Too many people who expected me to fail. So I went north. The Ivies were doing a drive to increase their Southern students. We had our own informal name for it," she told him and grinned.

"Which was?"

"'The gathering of the peasants,'" she told him. "We didn't get invited to the supper clubs or go yachting, but it was an amazing opportunity for a first-rate education."

"Then you came back."

"I did," she said simply as they neared the garage. She pointed to a shelf that held neatly set tools. "Kids need role models. They need to be inspired. They need love. So I came back. Did you get the schedule changes you needed to help coach the teams?"

He nodded as he set the tools down. "Amid a lot of dirty looks and turned backs and maybe even a gravy-train reference. Or two."

"I don't know what that is."

"Riding the gravy train. Not pulling your weight."

She turned to him with a look of commiseration. "Mike, I'm sorry. That's not fair."

It was, kind of, because the guys only knew what they saw: that a newcomer to their department was already getting favors the first week on the job. "They'll give me a second chance, I expect. After a while."

"You saved Coach's life."

"I *helped*," he corrected her.

"You got there before the EMTs," she asserted. "I know because the boys gave me a complete play-by-play last night. I didn't want them going to bed without sharing their feelings."

"That's such a mom thing," he told her, and she burst out laughing. Once again, it felt good to see her laugh. Make her laugh.

"It is. I'm pretty sure the boys talk just to humor me."

"While wondering when they can get back to the stash of cookies hidden in the freezer, right?"

She turned, surprised. "You've been in my fridge?"

He shook his head. "It's a mom trick. But since frozen cookies are really good, kids figure it out pretty quick. Especially boys. We're always hungry." They were nearing the house so he got to the point of his visit. "I came over because I was wondering two things. First, I can take the boys to practice for you, if that's a help. We're going to the same place, so it's silly for us to both go. Second, my football info says you're chairing the fundraising event next month. Can we sit down and talk about that?"

Her brows shifted up. "Our coaches generally don't get involved with fundraising."

He made a dubious face. "Why's that?"

She shrugged. "They're generally working and coaching."

"That sounds a whole lot like their time is more valuable than yours, and that's not how I did things in Nashville. I helped lead, the kids pitched in, had a good time and realized their mothers weren't their gophers. They were leaders and partners. If you don't mind my butting in?"

Mind?
Did this nice guy have any clue what his offer meant?
Probably not.
"Why would I mind?" She took a deep breath that

made the shoulder of her T-shirt slip. She shoved it back into place and accepted before he had time to rethink his offer. "That would be wonderful. I'll see if Jordan's free to ride herd over here sometime in the next day or two so we can look at ideas for the fundraiser."

"I'm free the next two mornings," he told her.

"Then tomorrow morning works as long as Jordan's available. I'll text you. And offering a ride is great," she went on. "Hannah seems invested in long, drawn-out transitions. That doesn't cut it when there are three siblings with schedules. So, yes, your offer is wonderful. Will driving the boys mess things up for them?"

He looked puzzled. "How so?"

"Riding in with the coach? Favoritism? Like your change in scheduling request?"

"I've got laps at my disposal."

She frowned. Then it dawned. "Running laps for misbehavior."

"Yes, ma'am. A highly effective tool in the coaching arsenal."

"But not in the sheriff's department."

He smiled slightly. "Not as yet."

"Pity."

His smile grew and for a moment she was tempted to share Isaiah's concerns, that some of the kids weren't playing the game right. He hadn't called it cheating, exactly, but she'd read between the lines. Then again, Isaiah was more sensitive to things and if there were some underhanded things going on, a guy with Mike's experience would figure it out on his own. She moved toward the door. "I'll send the boys over. What time is good?"

"Five forty. They can help me get the equipment out of the shed."

"Perfect. And, Mike?"

He'd just started down the driveway. He paused and turned.

"Thank you. It really is a big help." After yesterday's hour-long fiasco, his offer was a gift. The football program entailed five nights of practice every week until the season began the first week of August, and a nightly struggle with Hannah wasn't a great transitioning tool. Having Mike take the boys gave her the gift of time to ease Hannah into their busy schedule.

"Glad to help. They're good boys."

The boys *were* good, but the remark was a solid reminder. Her romance-deprived brain thought he wanted to help her, personally, and that seemed special.

She should have known that a guy who loved football enough to coach was focused on the game and the players. Not on the players' forty-five-year-old mother.

I thought we were over the dating thing, Sugar.

Her mental scoldings always called her "Sugar," like one of her foster mothers used to. That foster mother had been one of the kind ones. They'd stayed in touch until she'd passed away about four years ago.

The mental reminder hit home.

Carly had given up men in favor of motherhood, but that was before Mike Morris had moved in across the street. There was no denying the attraction. He was handsome, kind, firm and funny. And the guy had a working brain. She loved that. If she'd been listing qualities on a dating app, Mike checked every box.

But getting involved with a neighbor spelled disaster and she didn't want anything disastrous in her life. Once was enough. Better to appreciate a good neighbor she could rely on than risk fallout.

When he pulled out of his driveway with the boys about forty minutes later, she was in the front yard with the girls. Jordan had agreed to babysit the next morning. She'd texted Mike the time and settled in to weed the three small front gardens.

Hannah was on the tire swing. Gracie was playing with toys on a blanket in the grass.

Mike paused the SUV and tooted the horn once he'd pulled out of his driveway. When she turned, he flashed a smile of appreciation at the girls, then flashed her a thumbs-up.

She smiled back. Her original plan for a family had been two parents and a couple of cute kids. When things hadn't worked out with her husband, she'd changed the ratio to 1:2 by adopting her sons.

Now it was 1:4 and she couldn't deny that having help was wonderful as long as she kept her emotions in check. Easy to say, not so easy to do, because every time Mike Morris flashed that smile, he eroded corners of her resolve.

Her phone rang as he drove off. Janice Sawyer's name flashed in the display. Janice was the social worker who'd handled the children's adoption placements. She took the call quickly. "Janice, hey. What's up? And why are you still working, it's nearly six o'clock."

"It's Gracie, Carly."

Carly frowned. "I don't understand."

"Lida Gables is petitioning the court to regain rights to Gracie."

Carly's heart clenched. For a moment, it seemed hard to breathe. Or to think. This couldn't be happening. Shouldn't be happening.

"That's impossible." She half sputtered the words as she tried to wrap her head around what Janice had said. "Gracie's adoption will be final next month. You can't be serious," she exclaimed, because how could this be real? How could this be possible? "Would the courts consider this in light of her chronic substance abuse?"

"She's claiming she stayed clean throughout the pregnancy and has been able to stay clean since delivery. She says that gives her the right to parent her own child."

Carly stood, stunned, but kept her voice soft so she wouldn't frighten the girls. "She stayed clean because she was in prison," Carly whispered. "I'm happy she's maintained her sobriety, but this can't be happening. The papers get signed in a few weeks. I've done everything that's been asked of me and she's never even asked to see Gracie. Or the boys. And there's no record of her ever even acknowledging Hannah in Sevierville County. What kind of judge would risk putting a beautiful child back into a questionable environment?"

"One who follows the law." Regret deepened Janice's tone. "If a parent successfully changes his or her ways, the Family Preservation Act says parental rights can be restored."

Carly paced the yard in disbelief.

Hannah was watching her, eyes wide. Did she sense Carly's discomfort?

Probably, which meant Carly had to keep a lid on rising emotions. "How do I fight this? Not because I have anything against Lida Gables, but because I can't imagine anyone wrenching Gracie out of my arms and into a situation that could rapidly deteriorate once the reality of raising children sets in. Then we have a repeat of Isaiah and Isaac's early childhood trauma."

"I don't disagree," Janice replied. "We are opposing the petition, but this could go against you, Carly. If the adoption were final, that would be different."

"Does this mean Hannah's at risk, too?"

"No. She doesn't want Hannah. She's made that quite clear. She said her relationship with Hannah's father is nothing to be remembered and she wants nothing to do with that child."

Carly's pulse spiked higher. *That child.* "She said that?"

Janice sighed. "She did."

The phrase stung. She'd heard those words repeatedly for over a decade. *Who's* that *child? What are you going to do with* that *child? Is* that *child coming along?* The familiar phrasing still sent a coil of anger up her spine.

But she was the adult now, making her own way, her own choices. She was also a protector, and Gracie deserved every ounce of protection she could offer. "I need a lawyer."

"Can you afford one, Carly?"

"I can't afford *not* to have one." Giving Gracie up without a fight wasn't possible. She'd been Carly's baby from the time she was four days old. Carly had only held a handful of babies up to that moment when she nestled Gracie in her arms and their eyes met. She wasn't well off, but she did have a modest savings account from the sale of the house she'd owned with her ex-husband. "I'll get on that ASAP."

"I'll keep you apprised of the situation. The judge may want to meet with you prior to hearing the case. Or he may just rule on point of law."

"You mean without meeting me? Or Lida? Or the kids?"

"It's a possibility. I'm sorry, Carly. This caught me off guard, too. Lida was so sure that she was doing the right thing even before Gracie was born that I never expected this."

"I can't hate her for that, Janice," Carly replied. "But I'm not giving in, either." She took a deep breath.

Hannah had jumped off the swing. She was standing there in a cute romper, hands clasped in front of her, and her pensive expression put Carly on guard. "Gotta go."

"All right. I'll be in touch soon."

Hannah glanced right. Then left. As if looking for something.

Carly didn't approach her. She sat and patted the ground next to her. Gracie was rolling around on the blanket. She hadn't mastered crawling, and commando-creeping cramped her style, but she could roll her plump little self across a room in record time, so she was content to roll, check out soft toys and roll some more.

Carly patted the ground again. "Come see Mama, darlin'."

Hannah frowned. Again her gaze darted right, then left.

Then Gracie spotted her big sister. She sat up and squealed in joy. She bounced in excitement, chubby arms raised, and squealed again, as if calling Hannah over.

Hannah hesitated.

The pain in her little face broke Carly's heart. If love and comfort, and good food and nurturing could break through Hannah's armor, then it would happen, but as Hannah watched her baby sister, her face transformed.

Her eyes softened. She didn't look so worried. She looked almost interested, as if the baby's joy was something to be explored.

Carly stayed quiet.

Hannah hadn't taken to her or the boys yet. Only to Mike.

But as she began to cross the yard toward her baby sister, Carly breathed a sigh of relief. Hannah didn't have an easy trust of grown-ups or other kids, but it was quite clear that Gracie not only didn't pose a threat, she offered joy. And little Hannah Gables could use every ounce of joy she could get.

That only made Carly more determined to keep this family together. No matter what the cost.

Chapter Six

She ran across the street early the next morning and rapped on Mike's door.

He opened it slowly. Stared at her. Then the clock behind him. Then at her again. "It's six thirty-seven."

"I know."

He frowned, yawned and frowned again. "What's wrong?"

"I can't meet to talk about the fundraiser."

His brows drew down deeper. "You came over to wake me up to tell me that?"

She'd been up for an hour. She swallowed hard. "I never even thought about the time. Sorry. I forget that not everyone works on Carly time."

He swung the door wider. "Come in."

"Can't, the kids are asleep and I just didn't want to mess up your morning."

His incredulous look said she may have already done that, but his voice invited confidence. "Are the kids all right?"

"Yes and no. Their biological mother has filed a petition for custody of Gracie. I found out last night while the boys were at practice."

That woke him up. "She wants to take her back? After all this time?"

"Yes, and I can't think about anything else," she admitted. "I have to find a lawyer. A family lawyer. I have to see what my options are. I have to—"

He interrupted her. "My brother Sean."

It was her turn to be puzzled.

"Sean's a family lawyer in Newport. He handles adoptions, wills, normal stuff. And his rates are reasonable."

She wasn't sure if she believed that last part, but just knowing he was Mike's brother helped bridge the gap of who to trust. "Is he available? The lawyer I used for Gracie's initial paperwork retired and he was a one-man show. I didn't worry because I thought we were good to go, but we're not, and I need to know what my rights are. More importantly, what Gracie's rights are."

"Head back home until the sun's been up for another hour or so."

She flushed because dawn came later on the western side of the mountains.

"I'll get you and Sean connected while we're talking about the fundraiser, all right? You can trust him, Carly. Sean's one of the good guys. I promise."

The confidence of Mike's words took the pressure off her heart. "You're sure he's available?"

"Well, I'm his brother and I'm three inches taller and twenty pounds heavier, so I've got muscle on my side." He smiled.

His smile relaxed her even more. "I'll be back." She moved to the steps. "Eight thirty, right?"

"Gives me time for coffee, a run and a very important phone call."

"See you later."

Jordan had jumped at the chance to watch the kids while Carly grabbed coffee with Mike to chat about the football fundraiser. "To give you time to gaze into the eyes of the handsome guy across the way? Sugar, I will make time for that," she'd declared the day before. "I've got a ten-thirty appointment to examine finance options for the old hardware store, but I can be at your place at eight thirty. Where are you guys meeting?"

"His place," Carly told her. "There really is no place close by to grab coffee and talk. Not since the old diner closed. But I can't have a real conversation when we're constantly interrupted. He wants to help," she'd explained.

Jordan whistled lightly. "Just when you think it can't get any better."

"Stop," Carly scolded. Mike *was* the storybook hero type, but she wasn't looking for a hero. She'd been standing on her own two feet for a long time. "But I will love the help. It's been a challenge to find people able to jump in on regular things because everyone's been so tied up with recovery from the fire. Whatever ideas he has, they're welcome as long as helping hands come along with."

She popped over to Mike's house as soon as Jordan arrived.

He saw her coming and swung the wooden screen door open. "Come on in. I'm actually awake now."

She winced. "I forgot how early it was before. For-give me?"

She looked up.

Their eyes met. When they did, she didn't want to break the connection. Not now. Maybe not ever. The soap-and-water scent of him drew her. Fresh and clean, like a walk in the woods after a summer rain.

"Coffee's in the kitchen. Is that okay, instead of the porch? I figured a writing surface was important."

"It is and yes. And my tablet. Were you able to reach your brother?"

"He'll have the social worker send him the info and he'll set up a time to see you in the next couple of days. If you text him her name and number, he'll gather what he needs and go from there. Is that all right?"

It wasn't just all right. It was amazing. "It feels like I can breathe again," she confessed as she followed him to the kitchen at the back of the house. "Just knowing someone's on my side. Someone that knows the law. Thank you, Mike."

"My pleasure. Grab a seat. Ready for coffee?"

"Can't live without it and don't intend to try." She smiled as he brought two mugs to the table. "Those belonged to the Littletons."

"Yeah. I kept some of their big stuff and I'm keeping some of their kitchen stuff, too. The mugs were a no-brainer. Big. Good handles."

"We had many cups of coffee together with these mugs over the last five years," she told him. "I'm glad they're staying here with you. It's a nice reminder. Bo's illness turned their lives upside down in just a few weeks' time. That kind of thing is hard on folks. It didn't give them time to adjust."

"Life doesn't always go as planned."

He didn't meet her eyes when he said it, but she heard the note of regret in his voice.

"Did you bring old plans with you from Nashville?" She indicated the stack of papers on the table.

"Printed them from laptop notes. I wanted time to get settled in here before I brought things east. And we needed to move the Littletons' stuff out."

"True. Ah." She puffed a cooling breath over the mug's surface and smiled as she took her first sip. "Excellent coffee."

"Not too strong?"

"Is there such a thing, Mike?" With the mug raised, she lifted her eyebrows in disbelief then laughed when he laughed. "It's wonderful. So…whatcha got, Coach? Because we've only got a few weeks to pull this off, so if I'm changing things up, I want to get everything in order."

He splayed a handful of papers in front of her and she had to fight the urge to give him a kiss of thanks. He'd clearly been one hundred percent behind fundraising for his Nashville area teams and his notes made things look easy. When she got to the one that read "Sidewalk Sale" at the top, she grabbed it up. "This. This right here. This is perfect, Mike. We usually did a walk-in type thing on the church grounds, but this is ideal now."

He sat back. "And fairly simple if the shop owners agree."

"Oh, they'll agree," she promised. "We can get the

sports boosters, school moms and all the nonprofits involved because we have sidewalks now!"

He didn't try to mask his confusion. "I don't get it."

She laughed because he wouldn't get it, but she did. And she knew that the idea of a sidewalk sale would draw in locals because they were so happy with the look of the new business district center. It would attract tourists, too, and folks traveling from Newport to Gatlinburg or Pigeon Forge would go right through their town. "The sidewalks are new. It was part of Shane Stone's idea to revitalize the town after the fire. The vendors will love it, the booster clubs and nonprofits will jump on board, and we'll all do well. As long as it doesn't rain."

"Won't matter much if we make it a three-day event," he drawled. "Friday, Saturday and Sunday. And we'll be playing league games by then."

"Done." She sipped her coffee, happy with the idea but honestly wondering how to spin the multiple plates she already had in the air. "I'll get emails out to all the businesses and booster clubs. The fire department, the auxiliaries, anyone connected with anything."

"And I'll clear the security side of things with the sheriff," he told her. "That way we have a couple of extra people keeping traffic and parking smooth. Extra eyes are never a bad thing for an event."

"I wouldn't have thought of that."

"Teamwork." He smiled into her eyes. Right into them, and her heart literally felt like it was playing hopscotch in her chest. "And don't worry about a setup crew," he promised. "The boys will help with setup and takedown. If we rent a tent and get permission from the church, could we set up Hidey's Barbecue over there for the day? Does he have an extra smoker?"

The promise of the boys' help made a good thing even better. She nodded. "He does, a small one. He can use the big one at his location and serve from the smaller setup. Want me to check with him?"

"I can do it. The guy makes the greatest barbecue I've ever had and we might as well put our best foot forward. If this goes well, it wouldn't hurt to make it an annual thing."

The thought of not having to reinvent the fundraiser every year appealed to Carly. "I love that idea."

He grinned and lifted his coffee mug to hers. "I'm completely in favor of saving time and effort."

She was, too. She bumped mugs with him.

His eyes crinkled. The mug brought out hints of amber in his eyes. Not enough to make the gray look green, but enough to brighten the tone.

She smiled back at him.

Carly pretended her pulse wasn't ramping up. She pretended her heart wasn't doing a silly dance in her chest, but she couldn't deny hoping his was doing the same.

They ironed out a few more details, then she checked the wall clock and stood. "Gotta get back. Jordan has to leave soon." She secured her electronic notebook under her arm and stuck out her hand. "Thank you, Mike. You have no idea what a help this is, especially this year. Not just offering your brother's help, but the coaching and the fundraiser. I really appreciate it."

He took her hand.

It felt right. Her hand in his, the touch of his skin on hers.

She didn't want him to let go. She wanted to stay right there, see where this might lead.

She didn't.

She shook his hand, smiled pretty and walked out the door.

Friends. Neighbors.

That was it because, in all truthfulness, her head and her heart couldn't handle one thing more.

Mike was pretty sure his heart had woken up that morning. Calling Sean, connecting him with Carly, hearing her concerns, feeling the urge to step in and save Gracie...

Yup.

They'd connected and he'd felt reenergized ever since. So when he saw three deputy sheriffs walk onto the field and stand near Brice Masterson that evening, he almost didn't care.

Brice wasn't just an offensive coordinator for a bunch of rural kids playing football. Mike had discovered that he was a Cocke County assistant district attorney with friends in the sheriff's department. Those three friends showed up at practice. They stood on the sidelines, a unified front he could be commanding in three months' time.

They didn't know that.

He did.

And while he appreciated their support of a friend they thought had been bested by an outlier, why weren't they trusting Coach Wynn's judgment? Unless there was something else going on?

He watched as the coaches ran drills, but stepped in when Brice went easy on one of the smaller players. The coach wasn't going to like Mike's interference.

Too bad. He trotted up the field and aimed a firm look at the boy. "Ralphie, here's the deal."

The boy looked up at Mike and swallowed hard.

"If you fade away from the play for any reason other than shifting your forward motion away from the defenders, you're benched. Use your size to your advantage."

The boy frowned.

Brice grunted in clear disapproval.

Mike ignored both. "You're smaller than the other guys. You can fit into places no one else can. Think about the best running backs you know. A lot of them are smaller guys because size isn't everything in football. Use your agility and your brains to put you in the right place at the right time. Don't wait to react. Anticipate. And be mentally prepared to be brought down because, I guarantee you, it's going to happen."

"Okay, Coach."

Ralphie hustled back to the sidelines and when he was included in a play a few minutes later, he didn't fade from the action. He feinted left, went right and gained seven yards. Mike would take a play like that all day long.

Masterson waited until the kids were on a water break to have his say. "Our goal here isn't to get kids hurt."

Mike kept his tone mild. "Our goal is to teach skills

and win games. The only way to do that is to utilize every player's strength."

"While putting them in peril?"

"Sometimes."

Masterson was clearly rattled. Mike wasn't. And that seemed to annoy the other man even more.

"Football's a perilous sport," Mike reminded the offensive coordinator. "Injuries happen. There's no getting around that for motivated athletes."

"Ralphie's got family stuff going on," Masterson pressed. "I cut him a little slack because the kid has enough on his plate. And his size *is* a factor."

"His size is only a factor if you make it a detriment," Mike replied. "If you make it an advantage, you put the power where it should be. In his hands. And while he's at the lower end of the allowable size for this age group, he's in the range."

"And if we cart him off on a stretcher?" Masterson shot back. "Because some hulking adolescent takes a shot on him?"

"Then we get him the best medical care available, folks clap as he goes off the field and the game goes on."

Masterson looked disgusted.

Mike didn't care.

In his experience, more kids got hurt by being unprepared than from the normal motions of the game. Ralphie had heart. The kid wanted to do well, but when adults second-guessed abilities, self-doubt set in. Mike didn't know any better way than a solid sports experience to keep kids on the straight and narrow.

The assistant DA might not like Mike. He might not respect him, but Mike had been handed the reins by the coach, and then by the youth football board that oversaw the intercounty league.

He moved over to check the progress of Isaac's team.

Isaiah was a quiet leader on the older boys' squad. He wasn't huge. He was tall and lean, with an inner strength that would continue to grow.

His younger brother, Isaac, was a firestorm ready to erupt. He was the kid the opposition didn't want to make angry because Isaac drew on every ounce of his being to meet the opponent play for play. In fact, the Under 11 team had a handful of boys like that, which meant they might have to be reined in at times, depending on the circumstances.

An unfamiliar new player jogged Mike's way. The kid held a bunch of papers in his left hand, proof that the league board had approved his play.

And then the kid pulled off his helmet.

Not his.

Hers. The new walk-on was a girl.

She was almost as tall as Isaiah and she tucked her helmet beneath her arm as she extended a hand to Mike. "Coach, Tabitha Adams reporting. I'm a kicker and special teams' receiver."

The first thing Mike thought was that Masterson and the others had planted the girl to see how he'd react. Then she motioned toward the renovated business district. "My dad works with Mr. Stone. He's the guy rebuilding the town. I ride horses and I play football. I'm good at both, sir. I just got into town three days ago, that's why I missed the first week of practices."

The Under 13 coaches were watching him.

Masterson smirked.

That spurred Mike into action.

He took the girl's paperwork and clasped her hand. "Welcome aboard, Tabitha."

"Most folks call me Tabby, but I'll answer to anything, Coach. I just want to play."

"Head over to Coach Ben on the far line. He covers defense and special teams. I'll introduce you to the other players and coaches when we're done. And, Adams…," he added firmly, "this is your only pass. If you're late again, you owe me laps. One for every minute you're late."

"Got it, Coach."

He made good on his promise and introduced Tabitha to her teammates during the next water break. Her presence unnerved some of the boys and seemed to interest others, and that could be a whole new dynamic he hadn't faced before.

As practice broke up, Masterson and the other coaches approached him.

"Coach, are you really okay with this?" asked one of the younger coaches. He wasn't antagonistic, but his concern was obvious.

A part of Mike wasn't okay with it. His protective side had kicked into high gear when she'd pulled that helmet off to meet him. But Carly's words came rushing back to him, how she'd played baseball because keeping girls out of baseball was ridiculous.

Football was different, but the concept was the same.

He motioned to the sheaf of papers sitting on his duffel bag. "She's got great stats from Maryland."

"Until she gets hammered and we face a lawsuit," said Masterson. "We've never had a girl on a team before. Isn't that what cheerleading and gymnastics are for? That's girl-friendly stuff. Not a bone-crushing game like tackle football."

"If she can handle the drills and the hits and the ball, she stays. Every kid deserves a chance."

One of the younger coaches from Isaac's team posed a question and Mike appreciated his respectful approach. "Coach, I know you were a great player, and my sister over in Nashville says you were an awesome coach—her boys played in your program there. But this is different."

"How so?" he asked as Carly came their way with a stroller. Hannah was walking alongside, quiet and demure, until she spotted him. Then she raced toward him, arms out. Her look of glee grabbed hold of him. He scooped her up as the coach replied.

"She's a girl." He blurted the words as if not sure how else to say it. "I mean, it might be okay for the moment, but these boys are going to start exceeding her in weight and muscle mass and sheer upper body strength."

"That could be. But that's not the case yet, so let's give her the shot she deserves, as part of a team. The kid just rolled into town. Let's make her feel welcome."

Hannah had thrown her arms around him and clung. He patted her back and held her as the gathered men tried to figure out who she was, and why she was there.

Not their business. And he had to get to work, since he was on patrol until 1:00 a.m., part of the trade-off he'd made with the sheriff so he could coach the team.

"It's preposterous." Masterson didn't hold back. "We all know it, but everyone's afraid to say no these days. This isn't safe for her or the boys."

"A girl on special teams doesn't put additional risk on the boys," Mike replied. "It might inspire the guys to up their game to protect their kicker. We've already got a first-string kicker, correct?"

Coach Ben nodded.

"Unless she outperforms him, she'll be second string, which limits her playing time. But again." He pointed to the paperwork Tabitha had brought along. "The kid's good, so our first-string kicker will have to work hard to keep his spot."

"Nothing wrong with that," declared Coach Ben. "Players that earn their spots take better care of their spots."

Those were sage words to end on. "See you all tomorrow."

Carly had gotten closer. The familiar ponytail hung out the back of a ball cap, and the way she moved, as if life were free and easy, drew him because that wasn't her norm. Or his. Her smile made him want to smile in return, and there was something intrinsically linked between her expression, his smile and the child he held in his arms.

Carly's life wasn't easy and yet she carried herself like a champion while working to merge five people into a new family.

Isaiah came his way, too. "Thanks for the ride here, Coach. Mom, I'm going to take my stuff to the car, okay?"

"Yup." She tossed him the keys. "Throw all the gear into the trunk, all right? So we have enough room for everyone?"

His face shadowed, but he nodded. "Sure." And as

he jogged across the grass with his gear, he yelled to Isaac, "I call shotgun!"

"It's my turn!"

"Too slow."

"Mom!"

She ignored the exchange. Her eyes held shadows, but she smiled at Hannah in Mike's arms. "This one appears to have found safe refuge, which makes you a hero, Coach Morris."

He wasn't anyone's hero, but when he noted the concern behind Carly's smile, he wanted to be. Then Gracie banged her jingling toy up and down on the stroller tray.

The noise of the bells inside made her giggle. She grinned up at him, seeking approval, and the two tiny front teeth added a whole new level of cuteness, but all he could picture was the baby he'd lost. The boy he'd never had a chance to hold. To cuddle. To know.

Gracie wanted love, like every baby. But was it fair to her if every time he saw her he thought of his lost son?

Was he using his late son, Wyatt, as a crutch? Was he using his grievous losses to avoid future heartbreak?

Hannah backed her little face away from his neck. She smushed her two small hands against his cheeks and pressed a kiss to his face.

His heart melted.

He shifted her onto his hip and grasped the remaining bag with his free arm. The players had loaded equipment into the shed. Mike made sure the padlock was secure and started for the parking lot with Carly at his side.

It felt good.

He'd forgotten what good felt like, but the mix of

family, beautiful weather and football was definitely a winning combination.

"I hear you've got a girl on the team."

He sidled a look down at Carly. "That only just happened. Word travels fast."

"Hazards of living in a small town. The football moms have a group text I'm a part of. There are a lot of mixed emotions, I can tell you. Should be interesting. As if you didn't have enough on your plate right now." She indicated Masterson and his buddies as they left the parking lot.

"She can kick. And run. And it's your fault I said yes so quickly," he told her.

"It's always the woman's fault, isn't it?" she quipped. Her sass made him smile, and that felt good, too.

"My mother would argue with that. For kids, it's always the mother's fault, and for the moms, it's the husband's fault. It all comes down to perspective."

Carly laughed. "I like your mother. She's got common sense."

"She does. Hopefully passed it on to her kids. Guys," he addressed the two boys, "whose turn is it to ride up front?"

"Mine."

"His." Isaiah slid out of the seat and let Isaac take it. "But he's such an easy target, Coach."

"Save your targeting for the field and don't tease your brother," Carly ordered. "Isaiah, can you adjust Hannah's booster seat so we can get her strapped in?"

"Barely."

The boy was right. The back seat of the midsize sedan was advertised as room for three, but two car seats overruled the claim. By the time they had the girls into their seats, Isaiah was wedged almost sideways between them.

"I'd run the boys home if I could," said Mike. "But I've got to head straight back to Newport."

"Zay." Isaac turned in the front seat. "I can fit back there better. You can have my turn up here."

Isaiah reached up and ruffled Isaac's hair. "It's fine, dude. All good. But thanks for offering," he told Isaac, then turned his attention back to Mike. "Thanks again, Coach."

"Yeah, thank you!" Isaac fist-pumped the air outside his window as they pulled away, and as Mike piled his duffel into the back of his SUV, another bit of reality tweaked him. He had no money worries, no space worries, no food concerns.

Carly didn't seem to be hurting for money, but she'd taken time off from teaching until the end of Christmas break. What did that mean for her income? Then a pricey lawyer thrown in on top of that?

That night on patrol, he studied the layouts of roads and homes surrounding him. Cocke County lay along the Great Smoky Mountains National Park, with the quiet mountain ambience of Eastern Tennessee, so different from what he was used to in Nashville and the surrounding area. The original Kendrick family homestead wasn't far from Newport. The house and farm were rented out now. Sean managed the rental property but he'd mentioned a couple of times that it was tying him down too much now that his kids were older. If Mike stayed, maybe he could give Sean a break.

By the time he pulled into his driveway at 1:20 a.m.,

all was quiet and dark in the house across the street. No music wafted from the porch, and the outside lights cut a ribbon of brightness through the night. It seemed right to glance that way, to make sure everything was in order.

He made his way inside and didn't bother turning on any lights. He went upstairs and fell asleep in the gear he'd worn to practice.

He'd said he wanted to be tired enough to sleep.

Tonight he was.

Chapter Seven

The only way to keep her mind off this new twist with Gracie was to keep busy, but sweltering heat and humidity left too much time to think about what might happen.

Jordan called at just the right moment. "Do you guys want an amazing project for this weekend?"

Carly didn't even have to ask what it was. She jumped in quickly. "Yes."

"The estate sale at your neighbor's place is Friday and Saturday. Humidity is supposed to drop and the hunky cop has some shade trees. The boys could make a killing with a baked goods and lemonade stand."

With the air-conditioning going, baking wouldn't be so bad. "You're a lifesaver."

Jordan laughed. "I knew it was a good idea, but didn't think it had potential lifesaving capabilities. My bad. Why do you need lifesaving?"

The conversation about Gracie couldn't happen with kids in the house, so Carly kept it generic. "Trying to keep kids busy in the heat is tricky. The boys will love creating things, then selling them, then having money in their pockets. It's a total home run, Jordan."

"Then I'm happy I called. The sale starts at 10:00 a.m. on Friday, but there are always a few early birds trying to sneak a peek."

"We'll be ready." She hung up and called the boys into the kitchen. Hannah was in a corner of the living room, stacking plastic locking blocks, and as soon as she made a tower, Gracie would roll her way and knock them down.

Gracie thought it was the best gig ever.

Hannah was not amused.

Carly tucked Gracie into her walker. That way she was mobile but couldn't reach Hannah's creations. If Hannah changed positions, though, Gracie would have another clear shot, so Carly set up two sections of toddler fencing. That kept the sisters near each other but made sure Hannah's work was safe from Gracie's search-and-destroy mentality.

"We're going to do a mega bake sale and lemonade stand at Mike's house."

Isaiah arched a skeptical brow. "And why would we do this on a road with no traffic except us and him?"

"Jordan is staging a big sale over there on Friday and Saturday," she explained. "It should draw a lot of people, and you get to keep all the profits."

The boys' eyes went wide.

"We need to start baking today, though, if we're going to pull this off properly. And I'll bake on Friday while you guys run the stand."

"But we don't have a stand," Isaac noted.

"Sure do." Carly hooked a thumb toward the garage.

"Tables and a pop-up tent. We've got all you need right out there. I'll keep an eye on the girls here and you gentlemen can handle the selling end."

"I'm good at selling things," boasted Isaac. "Remember those cards last year?"

Carly nodded. He'd had two dozen football cards that a classmate wanted, and he'd sold them for ten dollars. Thrilled with his first successful sale, her younger son had been embracing the thought of being an entrepreneur ever since. "This gives you a chance to sell lots of stuff, buddy."

"Can we take turns?" asked Isaiah.

"In this heat? Yes. But if it's really busy, which happens a lot on the first day especially, you should both be there. I'll grab lemonade mix and anything else we might need while you guys are at practice tonight."

"Can we sell sweet tea, too?" suggested Isaac. "You know folks'll love that."

"Great idea."

The rest of her day was filled with baking.

Isaiah helped her in the morning, but he went swimming at a friend's house in the afternoon. Isaac jumped in wholeheartedly, and by the time they were ready to go to practice that night, they'd made three kinds of cookies that were now wrapped and tucked into the small freezer in the garage. She did save a tub of cookies for practice. If there was anything teen and tween boys loved, it was food.

Janice's text came through shortly before seven that evening. *Petition for full custody filed. No timeline. I'm so sorry.*

Full custody.

Gracie was playing on a blanket to Carly's left. She babbled and laughed and even waved now. That was a new trick. She delighted people with her bright smile and that funny, awkward wave.

She couldn't imagine letting Gracie go. Not that she didn't sympathize with Lida, but Carly knew herself. She wouldn't have gone into any of this if she'd thought a child would be wrenched away. She knew better than to set herself up for that kind of emotional breakdown. If Gracie had been a foster care placement, that would be different, but she wasn't. She'd been fully released for adoption, only now…

Tears gathered.

She blinked them back then pressed the backs of her hands to her eyes. She couldn't cry here. She'd cry later. And if she had to remortgage the house to pay Sean Morris's legal fees, she would.

Lida Gables had given her the greatest gifts, but Carly had doubts. Maybe Lida would stay clean. Maybe she wouldn't. Either way, the baby's future shouldn't rest on uncertain ground. Carly knew enough about the system to know that if Lida regained custody, it would be a long, time-consuming task to get it back if things went bad.

She held it together until the kids were in bed.

Then she went outside and cried.

Sean called Mike the following morning. "This isn't good news," he told him. "Nothing about this custody case is going to be easy."

Mike had been afraid of that.

Sean continued. "Precedent and the law puts the

mother in the driver's seat, even with past abuses, because the key word a judge has to look for is 'past.' If she's clean, that makes a huge difference in the judge's latitude."

"So this could go against Carly, even though she's had the baby for eight months?"

"That's your new neighbor, right?"

"And a friend," Mike added then wondered why he'd done it. Sean would have been fine with the term "neighbor."

"I'll call her later this morning. Have her meet with me whenever she can get a little time away from the kids. They don't need to hear any of this."

Mike thought of Isaiah's thoughtful nature. Isaac's quick protective reactions. How they'd feel knowing their sister was still wanted by their mother while they'd been abandoned. How does a kid handle that mentally and emotionally?

Not well, he knew. "Go pro bono on this, Sean," Mike instructed. "I'll cover the bill, but Carly doesn't need to know that. I want her to think you're just a Good Samaritan who likes helping kids."

"Instead of thinking you're the good one?" The tone of Sean's question spiked up. "Michael, there's only one reason in the world a guy does this and doesn't take credit. It's because he doesn't want to give the lady the wrong idea."

"Or he's humble and kind."

"Tell me this. Why don't you want her to know you're footing the bill? You know I can do this gratis. I do it all the time."

"You manage enough family stuff with the house

and the farm," Mike replied. "Let me take care of this. I'll call in a favor another time."

"Whatever you say. Gotta go. Client time."

Mike hung up. He was doing split shifts this week because there hadn't been enough people to cover the late-night schedule. Next week he'd be on early days; in at five in the morning, off at two in the afternoon. That gave him some time to take care of the house and yard. And football.

As he walked out onto the broad porch, he could see a portion of Carly's house and driveway.

He'd stepped into a lot of drama by moving here, and not drama of his own this time. He'd waded into a convoluted family dynamic that drew him.

You mean she *draws you. The kids are a bonus.*

There was truth in that, but there was another truth as well. He wasn't ready to immerse himself in drama of any kind. Sometimes at night, when he'd wake up in a cold sweat, he wondered if he'd ever be okay again. The irony of a sheriff being weak wasn't lost on him. He could polish his personal facade for the job. He could talk his way through situations because he was experienced and well trained. His professional life wasn't the problem.

His personal life was another story.

Just then, Isaac ran across Carly's driveway. He landed at an angle from the portable basketball hoop, set his feet and sent a fingertip-rolling shot into the basket. Nothing but net.

They were good boys. Who might have taken a different path in life if Carly hadn't stepped in.

Mike sucked in a deep breath.

He couldn't afford the attraction. He knew that. But he couldn't take the hit to his conscience that backing away would give him. Could he be a good friend and only a good friend?

He had no choice.

But—

Just sitting and talking with her yesterday morning had opened his eyes to a new chance, one he hadn't thought possible. Was he healed enough to move forward? Or too scarred and afraid to test the waters?

You're being ridiculous. Do more. Think less.

He'd gotten where he was professionally by using wisdom, experience and intuition. It was time to start doing that in all aspects of his life again.

Chapter Eight

Mike grabbed some quick groceries before the morning sale began. He came up the road about ten forty on Friday morning, crested the knoll and stopped.

Cars clogged access along both sides of the road. A vehicle was coming his way. There was no room for his SUV to fit, so he pulled over, let her go through, then eased his SUV along the narrowed strip of road and pulled off onto his grass once he got close enough. Furniture and other stuff made the driveway inaccessible, and people milled everywhere.

The sale had started less than an hour ago, and the boys were frantically selling cookies, pouring sweet tea, making change and sending worried looks across the street. "What's wrong?" asked Mike as he stepped into their pop-up tent area.

"Mom's supposed to be bringing more stuff, but she hasn't." Isaiah spoke softly.

Customers were examining the items Jordan and her team had placed outside, and more folks were inside the house, checking things out. Mike tried to ignore how odd that felt. People roaming around his house. Even though it wasn't really his. Not yet, anyway. Even with Nothing For Sale In This Room signs scattered around, the thought of people looking at his personal things was unnerving. "I'll run over and see what's going on."

"Thanks, Coach. I was gonna…" explained Isaac, his serious tone underscoring his concern and commitment, "but I didn't want to leave Isaiah with all these people."

"I'm on it, boys." He jogged across the street.

Gracie was in her walker in the living room.

Hannah was shrieking in Carly's arms. Carly had ducked her head close to Hannah's to prevent a head bonk, while big tears formed in Gracie's eyes.

"What's happened?" he asked.

Hannah tried to dive out of Carly's arms.

Carly didn't let her go. "No, not this time," she told the girl. "This time you stay with Mama and talk to me. Cuddle with me. Coach Mike is going to take things over to your big brothers for the bake sale."

She was right. And he knew it. He couldn't undermine her by always comforting Hannah, because he wasn't always there. But reality hit him.

He liked comforting the little girl. And when two big, fat tears fell down Gracie's cheeks, he reached over and gently wiped them away. Then he picked up the pacifier that had fallen to the floor, brushed it off on his pant leg and handed it back to Gracie. She latched on like a pro and stared up at him with big brown eyes.

Would Wyatt have had brown eyes eventually?

He'd never know, but Gracie gazed up at him with trusting eyes surrounded by thick black lashes. He wasn't even sure it was normal for a baby to have such pretty eyelashes and, when she blinked twice, he was pretty sure she was flirting with him.

"Earth to Mike." Carly was ignoring Hannah's outburst. She didn't try to talk over it. She spoke through it. "Cookie delivery, please."

"On it."

She indicated the kitchen island with her chin. He gathered up three trays of wrapped cookies. He took those across the street then came back for the fresh jugs of iced tea and lemonade.

He dropped those off for the boys, realized they were almost out of paper cups and brought two more sleeves over, along with two packages of paper towels.

By the time he was done running back and forth, Hannah had calmed down, Gracie was eating handfuls of cereal in her high chair, and the plastic fencing was set up, separating the two girls. "I see we've initiated solitary confinement," he whispered to Carly. "If the inmates can't get along—"

"Gracie wants to destroy everything Hannah makes," Carly whispered. "Do you think it will be like this forever? The correct answer is no."

"I've only got my family to go on, but I'd have to say it depends on both parties, and how forgiving they are. In other words, the jury might be out on this for a long time, Carly. A very long time." He grinned at her. When she sent him a mock frown, he wanted to pull her close and hug her.

He didn't.

But he wanted to.

He stepped back. "Anything else that needs to go over?"

"Not at the moment. Does that mean we get a coffee break now?" she asked.

He nodded. "Sounds great. Okay if I hang out here and run things over as needed?" he asked. "Then you can keep baking, the girls don't have to go out in this heat and the boys can run the show. Which they're doing quite well, by the way."

"That sounds wonderful because I didn't think I'd need to run interference with the girls quite so often. And you can't exactly go home, can you?"

It was on the tip of his tongue to say the Littletons' wasn't his home, but he didn't. He held back and agreed. "No, ma'am, I cannot. Want me to make the coffee while you scoop cookie dough?"

"Yes, please." She didn't waste time and when the oven timer dinged a few minutes later, she had two more trays ready to go in once two came out. He made coffee while she filled the counters with delicious cookies of all sorts, and when he realized she had dozens still thawing on the countertop, he was impressed.

"You prepped ahead."

"One of my foster mothers ran bake sales for her church every two months. We always baked up a storm ahead of time because kitchen ovens can only handle a couple of trays at a time. She taught me well."

"She sounds nice."

"That one was," she replied, which meant there were others who weren't so nice. "But then Daddy Joe got sick and she had to stop caring for kids. They're in Florida now, but they send me cards now and again. They haven't forgotten. Neither have I."

They spent hours with coffee, cookies and little girls,

and by the time the sale ended at four, the boys had made over a hundred dollars and Carly had stacks of cookies ready for the next day. And a sleeping baby, giving Hannah respite from standing guard over the few toys she allowed herself to play with.

Mike crossed the road to his house once Jordan's crew was done for the day. He took the boys to practice a little later and when Carly met them on the field at eight o'clock, they trudged toward the car. "They did great, but they're wiped out," he told her.

"The sale, the heat and the practice," she proposed.

"Yeah. I arranged a scrimmage with the Newport team for next Sunday here at our field. I thought that might help get word out about the fundraiser. Are the boys available to play?"

"As long as it's after church," she told him. "What time did you set for it?"

"Five. It will be cooler then. A little, anyway."

"Five works. And thank you for your help today. I didn't anticipate the trouble with the girls and you were a lifesaver."

"Well, it is kinda my job, ma'am." He winked.

She blushed.

He felt guilty for winking because he knew better than to flirt with a single mom.

But then she nudged him in the ribs with her elbow. "Knock it off."

He pretended confusion.

"I don't want to mess up our neighborly connection with silly romantic vibes that aren't going anywhere. We're old enough to know how badly that could end."

"You're right, of course."

She nodded, but he saw a glimmer of disappointment in her gaze. It disappeared, but was enough to make him think more about flirting. Smiling. Helping. "Of course, we do have to work side-by-side on the fundraiser, which throws us together on a regular basis for the next several weeks. So there's that."

"All business," she assured him, though the spots of color in her cheeks said something different. "Change of subject," she said then. "How's the estate sale going?" she asked as she pushed the stroller across the short, dry grass. Isaiah had Hannah's hand on one side and his duffel bag on the other. "I know it was busy. I must have had fifty cars turn around in my driveway."

"The downside of being at the end of the trail."

"Privacy and road safety are magnified when you're the last place on the block. And a country block, at that."

"True."

Isaac had reached the car and was stowing his pads and gear into the trunk. Isaiah was moving his way when his bag slipped from his shoulder. He shrugged up to reverse the momentum, and when he did, his grip on Hannah must have loosened because she jerked free and raced into the parking lot, directly into the path of a car backing out of a parking space.

Carly screamed her name.

Isaiah dumped his bag and raced after her. Mike did, too, but he saw the inevitable before it happened as the vintage vehicle continued to move in reverse. The fin-backed classic car was too old to have rear cameras or alerts, and as Isaiah swerved left to grab Hannah out of harm's way, the left side of the old car clipped the boy.

He went down.

Mike's heart went down with him. The thrust of the car wasn't too great, but it was enough of a jolt that Isaiah's lower half twisted. When it did, his right leg didn't twist with the rest.

He crashed to the pavement while thrusting Hannah toward Mike. Mike was just close enough to grab hold of Hannah to keep her from being hit.

She looked terrified. She leapt into his arms and ducked her head while Mike's heart sank. Isaiah looked up at him. Read his expression.

And then he looked down at the obviously broken leg and burst into tears.

Carly didn't have time to think. She dialed 9-1-1 instantly and reported the accident as if her heart wasn't breaking into a million pieces.

Hannah was bawling in Mike's arms. Isaac was, too. Mike had a firm grip on the younger boy while comforting Hannah.

One of the coach's wives had stepped in and was feeding Gracie a freeze pop. It kept her distracted and probably felt good on sore, teething gums.

"Kendrick Creek responding," the 9-1-1 operator assured her.

The ambulance whistle pealed through the muggy air as Carly cradled Isaiah's upper body.

Jess Bristol came out of nowhere with her medical bag. Her mother was with her. Carly took one look at Doc Mary, a woman who'd done so much for the community and was fighting a losing battle with cancer, and her vow not to cry until later hung on by a thread.

Mary didn't mince words as she knelt at Isaiah's side.

"You're my kind of man, Isaiah Bradley. You saved that little girl's life by stepping in the way you did. I know you're in pain, son," she went on, her tone firm and soft. "We're going to get you over to Newport and get this lined up right. If it's a clean break, they can put you into a cast in a few days and you should only miss half the season. The hot half, and that's something to be grateful for on hundred-degree days. Trust me, Isaiah."

Carly held Isaiah as he locked eyes with Doc Mary.

"I don't spin sunshine or throw shade," the aging doctor told him. "Most leg injuries come back one hundred percent. Don't be messing with my stats, okay?"

Her even tone soothed him. He grimaced with pain, but said, "I won't, Doc. We've got a title to win."

"You sure do, and I don't want those Northern Tennessee Tigers to be lauding it over us for two years in a row. Once was bad enough."

The ambulance pulled in.

The EMTs had Isaiah loaded within minutes.

Jess pointed out her SUV to Carly. "Let's trade cars. You've got the car seats in yours. I'll take the kids back to your house and get them settled. Shane's home with Jolie and Sam. You take mine to the hospital." She tossed Carly the keys.

Mike had called into the sheriff's office. He disconnected and faced Carly. "I'll follow you. Orrie," he addressed the driver of the vintage vehicle. "We'll have to take a police report. A deputy is pulling in now, so I'm going to have you talk to him, all right?"

"I know, I know, and it was all my fault," spewed the older man. "I craned my neck like always, but I didn't see anything behind those fins. Mother always tells me to pull in when I park, that the fins are a hazard, and I tell her she's just too short to see proper in a big old car like this. But she's right. I couldn't see, either. And I'm sorry, Carly." Tears streamed down the old man's cheeks. "So sorry."

He couldn't see and still backed up? A spike of anger thrummed down her spine. There were kids all over this parking lot at all times of day.

She couldn't reply to Orrie. Not now. She reassured Isaac, kissed him and the girls, and climbed into Jess's car. It was a twenty-minute ride to the medical center in Newport, too much time to think and more than enough time to be overwhelmed.

She'd been doing fine with the boys. Just fine. Why did she think it wise to rock the boat? Take on more? What was she thinking?

The adrenaline rush made her head ache.

She wasn't a superhero.

She wasn't experienced in mothering. Far from it, so why did she—

Be still...be still...and know that I am God.

The gentle words came from the Christian station on Jess's car radio right then, exactly when Carly needed those very words. That very line from a beautiful Psalm, a reminder of who was in charge.

Not her.

God.

Guilt hit her because she hadn't taken the time to bring the girls' fates to the altar, not like she had with their big brothers. So maybe it was still her fault for taking on too much, but—

She pulled into the parking lot adjacent to the ER,

jumped out of the vehicle and raced inside to her beloved son.

A nurse directed her to Isaiah's cubicle. He looked less stressed now.

"Pain meds," the nurse whispered. "We're taking him to X-ray in a few minutes, then the doctor will make sure the bones are lined up. He'll need to see an orthopedist early next week. We can give you a couple of names. Are you here alone?" she asked. "If you have someone else in the waiting room, I can let them know what's going on. We only have enough space to allow one person back here per patient," she added in apology.

"No one else. I'm it," said Carly, but less than ten minutes later, a deep, familiar voice sounded just beyond Isaiah's curtain. "Anybody in here need coffee?"

"Mike?" Carly had been holding Isaiah's hand. The meds had helped curb the pain, but he wasn't comfortable enough to doze off. She pulled back the curtain and stared at the tray of coffees in his hand. "Where'd you find coffee at this time of day?"

"I know the folks that run the coffee shop up Broadway. She was closing up, but I called in a favor."

"A frappe?" Isaiah's interest was piqued instantly when he saw the caramel-drizzled drink cup. "Is that for me, Coach?"

"All yours." Mike handed it over with a straw. Isaiah fumbled the straw a little and Carly reached in to help.

Mike cleared his throat. "It's your leg that's hurt, QB, not your arm. Open your own straw."

"Yessir." Mike's words made Isaiah sit straighter in the bed. "This is great, Coach. Thank you."

"You're welcome." He turned back to Carly. "How's the insurance situation?"

"Good coverage, small co-pay. One of the perks of working for the department of education."

"Good. I know how sudden medical bills can mess things up."

She wanted to ask how he knew, but it wasn't her business. She accepted the iced coffee, sipped it and sighed. "This is great coffee."

"Just cream, right? Because I haven't seen you put sugar in your coffee."

"Just cream," she told him, then realized that he'd paid attention to what she put into her coffee. Paid attention to her kids. Paid attention to her.

The realization warmed her even with the hospital's AC cranked up high.

A pair of techs arrived to move Isaiah to X-ray. She leaned down, kissed his brow and squeezed his hand. "I'll guard your drink."

He almost smiled. "Thanks, Mom."

And it wasn't until they wheeled him out of the room that she let the tears flow.

"Hey, now…" Mike gathered her into his arms for a big hug, the kind of hug that made her feel like he'd never let go. The kind of hug that felt good. So good. "You did it," he whispered into her hair. "You held it together until the kid was out of sight."

She batted his arm but left her cheek against his chest. "I wanted to cry from the very moment I saw what was going to happen and knew I couldn't stop it. What an awful feeling. I was right there. And couldn't prevent what happened."

"I know."

Something in his tone made her draw back.

He met her gaze. "The helplessness of the moment. I hate that," he admitted. "It's the worst."

"It is." She sighed and pulled away from the embrace. "I kept reliving it all the way here, wondering what I could have or should have done better because maybe I was foolish to take on the girls. I jumped in because the thought of them being off on their own, away from family, hit home with me. I didn't take time to think, to pray, to work things out. I acted. What if I shouldn't have?" she asked him outright. "What if I messed up by taking on more than I can handle?" She went on without giving him time to reply.

"That's what was running through my head," she continued, "until this song came on in Jess's car about how we should be still and know that God is God. And then it hit me that no matter how much I plan or think or work things out in my head, things will happen. Life happens. I can't fix it all. I can't plan for it all. And maybe the best I can do is make sure I react well. Maybe that's all any parent can do." She took a big sip of her coffee and raised the plastic cup up higher. "And have good friends to soften those rough edges. The kind that can call in favors with the coffee people and get a free pass into the ER because they're wearing a sheriff's badge."

He grinned. Winked. "Deputy, ma'am. But thank you for the promotion."

"Thank you for caring," she told him. "You barely got here before you hit the ground running for me, the football team and the sheriff's department. Thank you, Mike. I mean that so much. Just—" She raised her gaze and smiled softly into his eyes. "Thank you."

Chapter Nine

She made him feel like a hero.

He knew better. He knew the raw side of helplessness too well, but her words bolstered him. They made him want to be heroic, and he hadn't felt that way in a long while. "How's the coffee?"

"So good. And how did you know that Isaiah would like the frappe?"

"What kid wouldn't?"

His pager buzzed. He took a step back. "Gotta go. Let me know if you need anything, okay? And when they spring you from here."

"I'll call."

"Tell Isaiah I'll be by."

"I will."

His half shift was packed with back-to-back calls. Friday nights were always busy and he was working in the Newport sector this night.

Two hours later Carly's text came through. Heading home. Ortho on Tuesday. Break looks fairly simple.

He almost thanked God but stopped himself. Since his wife's and son's deaths, Mike had lost touch with Him.

He'd believed when he was young. As much as a kid could, he supposed. He'd accepted the idea of God and faith, and gone to church to please his parents, then his wife.

He hadn't been back in over two years.

When he pulled into the driveway of his house that night, he noted that Jordan's crew had draped tarps over the remaining outdoor items scattered throughout the yard. That created a series of eerie images, but he was too tired to care about tarps or dew.

He turned left to check Carly's house. It seemed quiet. No inside lights.

But as he opened his door, a thought niggled at him.

Was Hannah all right? It had to be traumatizing for a small child to be nearly hit by a car, to see another child hit and hurting, then be cared for by strangers.

He wanted to cross the road and double-check but what if he woke someone? And if he texted Carly, would he wake her, too?

He couldn't risk it. Morning was a scant six hours away. He went to bed. Sleep was a long time coming and when his phone alarm buzzed at seven, his first reaction was to throw it across the room and bury his head beneath the pillow.

He did neither and by eight thirty he'd gotten in a four-mile run, had three cups of much-needed coffee and was busily replotting his coaching strategies for next week's scrimmage. Losing Isaiah as quarterback left a gaping hole in his first-string lineup.

He was reconfiguring two plays when Isaac knocked on the front door. "Hey, kid. Come on in."

Isaac stayed in the doorway. "I just wanted to see if I could start setting up the stand now even though it's early, Coach. Mom said I should check with you."

Isaiah wouldn't be around to help today or tomorrow, yet Isaac was willing to carry on. Impressive. "Can I help?"

"I can do it," Isaac told him, but then he drawled, "Unless you've got some time, Coach."

"Glad to."

He helped wiped dew from the tables. Then they set things up the way they'd been the day before. But if today was as busy as yesterday, there was no way Isaac could handle the influx alone. They crossed the road together and went into Carly's house. Isaac commandeered a sturdy plastic kids' wagon, perfect for bringing the bulk of supplies across the street.

Isaiah was still in bed.

Hannah was in her corner, facing the wall, playing her lonely little game.

Gracie was in the high chair, banging a spoon up and down. Bright-colored cereal danced on the plastic tray with each downbeat of the spoon, and the dancing cereal made her laugh.

Carly smiled when she spotted him. She pointed to the counter. "Fresh coffee if you need some. And thank you again for last night, Mike. It helped."

"It helped me, too."

"I wondered about that." She set three trays of snugly wrapped cookies in his arms. "Maybe sometime we'll

Get ready to relax and indulge with your FREE BOOKS and more!

Claim up to FOUR NEW BOOKS & TWO MYSTERY GIFTS – absolutely FREE!

Dear Reader,

We both know life can be difficult at times. That's why it's important to treat yourself so you can relax and recharge once in a while.

And I'd like to help you do this by sending you this amazing offer of up to FOUR brand new full length FREE BOOKS that WE pay for.

This is everything I have ready to send to you right now:

Try **Love Inspired® Romance Larger-Print** books and fall in love with inspirational romances that take you on an uplifting journey of faith, forgiveness and hope.

Try **Love Inspired® Suspense Larger-Print** books where courage and optimism unite in stories of faith and love in the face of danger.

Or **TRY BOTH!**

All we ask in return is that you answer 4 simple questions on the attached Treat Yourself survey. You'll get **Two Free Books** and **Two Mystery Gifts** from each series you try, *altogether worth over $20*! Who could pass up a deal like that?

Sincerely,

Pam Powers

Harlequin Reader Service

Treat Yourself to Free Books and Free Gifts.

Answer 4 fun questions and get rewarded.

We love to connect with our readers!
Please tell us a little about you...

	YES	NO
1. I LOVE reading a good book.	◯	
2. I indulge and "treat" myself often.	◯	◯
3. I love getting FREE things.	◯	◯
4. Reading is one of my favorite activities.	◯	◯

TREAT YOURSELF • Pick your 2 Free Books...

Yes! Please send me my Free Books from each series I select and Free Mystery Gifts. I understand that I am under no obligation to buy anything, as explained on the back of this card.

Which do you prefer?
❏ **Love Inspired® Romance Larger-Print** 122/322 IDL GRDP
❏ **Love Inspired® Suspense Larger-Print** 107/307 IDL GRDP
❏ **Try Both** 122/322 & 107/307 IDL GRED

FIRST NAME   LAST NAME

ADDRESS

APT.#   CITY

STATE/PROV.   ZIP/POSTAL CODE

EMAIL ❏ Please check this box if you would like to receive newsletters and promotional emails from Harlequin Enterprises ULC and its affiliates. You can unsubscribe anytime.

LI/SLI-520-TY22

sit on that porch swing of yours and talk. Unless some-one buys it."

"Not a chance. I already bought everything on the porch. Why mess with a good thing?"

Her smile deepened. "Agreed. Isaiah should be hob-bling down the stairs soon. Between the meds and the injury, he crashed as soon as we got home last night and was still sound asleep a few minutes ago."

"What time is his appointment on Tuesday?"

"Ten fifteen."

"How about if I set up a quick meeting with my brother right after that? Or before? Whatever works for you. I can keep Isaiah busy while you talk with Sean."

She set her tanned hand atop Gracie's dark curls. "That would be great. Jordan's coming over to watch the kids. I'll ask her to stay longer if your brother's avail-able."

Isaac came through the front door. "I got the new tablecloths on, and Ms. Jordan said they're even more cheerful than yesterday's, but I don't even know how a tablecloth can be cheerful. That's just weird."

"She means it looks cheerful," Carly told him. She handed him a jug of lemonade. "Put this in the wagon and come back for the iced tea, okay?"

"Yup."

She looked worried as she watched him go out the door. Under her breath, she said to Mike, "It's a lot to ask a ten-year-old to take on a whole day of sales alone, but he insisted he'll be just fine. Of course, my guilt is growing. Isaac, are you sure you're going to be all right over there all alone?" she asked as he bounded back in the front door.

Gracie squealed when she saw him. Hannah pretended he didn't exist.

"Coach is helping me," he assured her. "And he said if we eat PB and J for lunch, we get to order supper. He'll go pick it up when everybody clears out."

She lifted her eyes to his. "Mike, that's so nice of you. Are you sure you've got the time?"

"Nothin' but time, little lady," he drawled intentionally to make her smile. It worked. "I figured a job well done deserves a reward, and I grabbed barbecue at Hidey's my second day here. Never had better in all of Nashville, and that's saying something because you know how we Tennessee folks are about our barbecue."

"Wars have been fought over such matters. And I know our Hidey has won a few barbecue cook-offs in our time."

"Deservedly. Come on, kid. Let's get these cookies and drinks set up. We're running short on time."

He spent the morning working with Isaac when it was busy and nearby when it wasn't.

Isaac brought in nearly a hundred dollars in sales.

He was pumped, and when he split the money evenly with Isaiah that evening, Isaiah pushed it back to him. "I couldn't help so I don't get the money. You did the work. You get the goods."

Isaac folded his arms in front of his chest. It was a great stance on and off the field. "We did this together. Me and you. So we split stuff. That's how we do things, Isaiah." He stared at his bigger brother.

Isaiah stared back. And then he smiled. "Thanks, dude. You're all right."

"I know." Isaac flashed a smile that showed off bright

white teeth against his summer tan. "Anyhow, Coach helped me all day and said he didn't even want any pay for it. And he's getting us supper, so I knew I should be nice, too. Besides—" he folded his half of the money to take upstairs "—we're bros."

Mike moved toward the kitchen as Isaac hurried to put his money away. "Nice moment there."

"They're such good boys. Different, but close. They hated being separated for a couple of years when they were younger. Were you like that with your brothers?"

"When we weren't beating on each other. Or stealing each other's socks. Or swiping white T-shirts with no stains."

Doubt furrowed her brow. "That was a thing?"

"A huge thing. Mom used to say 'first up, best dressed.' How long were the boys living apart?" He couldn't imagine someone hauling one or more of the Morris boys to separate homes without a fight.

"Two years. They were eight and six, and it was the first time they'd been separated, so it was rough. That's when I found them online."

"And reunited them."

A tiny smile quirked the right side of her mouth. "I'm hoping for the same thing with Hannah. I want to bridge that gap from caregiver to family. But I don't think it's going to be an easy road for that precious little girl."

"How do you keep them safe?" he asked her.

"By not stepping foot outside the house for half a dozen years? Safety in solitude?" She set aside a cookie tray. "I honestly don't know. Yesterday's accident rocked me, but the more I think about it, the angrier I get. Little kids will do unexpected things, but how could someone back up blindly like that, hoping no one is in the way? That can't be allowed to happen. This time it was a broken leg, but either one of them could have been killed if Orrie had been going faster."

"He was cited for several things." One look at her face said that wasn't enough. "And his insurance will cover Isaiah's bills."

Carly took a seat at the table. So did Mike. Isaiah had earbuds in, so he couldn't overhear their conversation.

"Does it cover the trauma?" she asked softly. "Does it ease the pain and suffering of an almost teenager looking forward to his football season? Medical bill coverage is fine, but that only scratches the surface. Who's going to protect the next person from something like this?"

"People make mistakes behind the wheel. Maybe it's that simple, Carly."

She shook her head firmly. "Orrie ignored the rules of the road to drive his old car because it looks cool. That's a carelessness I can't take lightly, Mike."

"You're right. But there is a ripple effect with every action we take, so you'll want to think about that before you press too hard. The deputy said the old fellow was devastated by what happened. Rightfully so."

She drew her brows down. "I want them safe. I want everyone safe."

He understood that concept well. "Bubble Wrap?"

She flushed. "I don't usually feel this way, but seeing that car start to move, Hannah rushing into the parking lot and then Isaiah lurching forward to push her out of harm's way—"

"It was tough."

"Yeah. It could have been much worse, and yet I'm still so angry that Orrie knew he had blind spots. He narrowly missed killing my kids. I don't know how to forgive that. And I certainly won't forget it anytime soon."

Mike understood quite well. He'd never had the chance to protect what he'd loved and lost. He stood. "I'm going to pick up supper. Miss Hannah?"

Her face lit up when he called her name.

"Wanna take a drive?"

Eyes wide, she jumped up and hurried around the plastic fencing erected to keep Gracie out of Hannah's way at least some of the time. She jumped into his arms. He looked back at Carly. "Is that okay with you, Mom?"

Hannah's face darkened. She sent Carly a steely-eyed look and buried her face in Mike's neck.

"I expect Hannah would love that," Carly replied. She'd seen the expression and ignored it. "Have fun, you two. Her car seat is in the back of my car, Mike."

"Got it. Isaac, you want to ride along, too?"

"Can we check the new store by Hidey's, Coach? Mom said I could get a BB gun because I'm ten now, and they might have them at the new farm store. If that's okay with you, Mom?"

"Totally depending on Coach's time frame," she said. "I think BB guns are the best way to introduce gun safety and hunting rules when you're raising a pair of country boys."

"My dad did that with all of us." Mike glanced at his watch. "We'll have fifteen minutes. If the store's too busy, we'll have to go back another time, okay?"

"Sure! Thanks, Coach! I've got my money in my pocket. But not all of it," he assured Mike and Carly.

"See you in a bit. With food," Mike added.

When Carly smiled, that hero feeling washed over him again. It was a simple thing, providing a meal, but it meant something to her and those kids.

Therefore it meant something to him.

Don't get dependent, even though he's helping with the kids, and the fundraiser, and he's the sweetest neighbor ever.

The mental warning popped into her head over a week later.

Despite working a full-time job and coaching the football teams, Mike had found time to stop by with little pick-me-ups for Isaiah. A deck of new cards. A bag of Isaiah's favorite candy. And even some playtime for Hannah. He'd brought supper twice and he'd stayed around to eat peanut butter and jelly sandwiches with the kids at lunchtime on several occasions.

Carly wasn't fooling herself. Having Mike around wasn't just nice. It was wonderful. But she couldn't put the kids in the middle of a romance that could go bad. They'd been through enough.

Hannah's reserve had lessened—marginally. The petition for custody of Gracie had been tabled while the judge and then the child advocate were both away on vacation, but Mike's brother had been candid. As long as Lida Gables was drug- and alcohol-free, she had the upper hand. The relinquishment papers could be overruled by the mother's change of heart, but Carly couldn't dwell on that. Worry, yes. Dwell? No. There was too much to do. And it wasn't that she hoped for Lida's relapse. She was glad the other woman was drug-free, but that didn't mean she was going to give up Gracie without a fight.

She took the boys shopping for new school clothes. They grabbed shorts, T-shirts, socks and a backpack each.

Then there was Hannah. Carly didn't think she was emotionally ready for kindergarten so she'd enrolled the almost five-year-old in pre-K for the coming year. That created a new problem. The meager clothes Hannah had brought with her weren't enough for school and play, but Hannah wouldn't go shopping with Carly, and Carly wasn't going to drag her into stores. They were at an impasse.

"Can't you just buy her clothes online?" Mike asked her that evening after practice. Once school was back in session, their practices would be scaled back to three per week with a game on Sunday, still a busy schedule for a mom and four kids.

"I can," Carly answered. "But I was hoping to have a fun trip with her. I wanted to start building a mother-daughter connection," she added once the boys went into the house for snacks. Mike was working days now and didn't mind bringing the boys back-and-forth to practice to save her the trip into town. "I want her to know I'll always provide for her. Care for her. And have fun with her. Picking out clothes can be special, especially for a mother and daughter. Except she doesn't feel like I'm her mom, so there's that."

"What about if I come along?" he suggested.

"That only feeds into her idea that you're always going to be there for her."

"Or it'll help build that transition you talk about whenever you use your teacher-speak," he shot back.

She laughed, rueful. "I do that, don't I? Sorry, it's a bad habit."

"Well I've got cop-talk, so as long as we understand each other, we're fine. I'm off at three and can be back here before four. What about tomorrow afternoon? We can go to Sevierville. Is there someone who can watch the other kids?"

"Normally, Isaiah could," she replied. "He took the babysitter's course last year. And he's amazingly responsible. But he can't do it with his leg injured. I'll see if someone's free."

"Let me know. Maybe if we do a few things together, Hannah will get the idea that you're not Public Enemy Number One."

"Not funny." But when she sent him a pretend glare and he laughed, she realized it was funny. And sweet. And maybe too endearing because she needed to have a firm line in the sand.

And yet this felt nice.

Jordan's niece stepped in to help with the kids, and at four o'clock the next afternoon, Mike, Carly and Hannah went shopping in Sevierville.

Hannah was too big to sit in a shopping cart and thought the stroller was babyish, but when her eyes spotted a cart shaped like a car…

A car she thought she was driving—

She climbed right in, all smiles.

After picking up four shirts, matching shorts, three cute activewear outfits, two sets of jeans and long-sleeved shirts, new underwear and socks, Carly was ready to call the trip a total success.

Then they stopped by the dress section. Carly brought over two choices. One had tiny flowers dotting the fabric, an old-fashioned look that had come back in style. The other featured sparkles. Hannah loved the sparkles on her unicorn pillows.

Hannah took one look at the dresses and burst into tears.

Her face transformed. She didn't just reach for Mike, she semi-crawled up the big deputy to have him hold her. "Hey, hey, precious. What's up? You don't like the dresses Mommy found? Do you want different ones?"

Carly was at a complete loss.

They'd done so well, but the sight of the dresses hadn't just sparked a fire. It had launched an inferno.

Mike had to take Hannah out of the store.

Carly put those dresses back and picked out two others. A little girl needed a couple of dresses for church or parties or even school. She grabbed fancy socks and tights, too. While she was in line to pay for everything, she got a text from Mike. All is well. Stop by the ice cream shop when you're done.

Twenty minutes later, she walked into she frozen custard store and saw Mike and Hannah having custards at a table. Hannah had finally relaxed.

Carly joined them.

Mike looked repentant. "Normally, I don't reward bad behavior," he whispered, "but she'd been so good that I didn't want to ignore that, although I didn't want to ignore the meltdown, either."

"That meltdown wasn't a kid being naughty," Carly

whispered back. "That was a kid in distress. You did fine, Mike. And I'm grateful."

"Would you like something?" He waved toward the counter. "My treat."

She didn't really want one. Hannah's reaction made Carly's gut go tight, but she wanted Hannah to be surrounded by normalcy so she nodded. "I'd love a raspberry and chocolate twist. The smallest size they have."

Mike grinned as he stood. "My favorite."

"Really?"

"Yeah. I like the raspberry with vanilla, too, but the chocolate-raspberry mix is number one in my book."

"Mine, too."

"Well, isn't that interesting?" He grinned then ordered her cone and brought it back to their small table.

Hannah sat by Mike's side. She barely looked at Carly, but every now and then she'd sneak a glance her way.

Carly pretended not to notice.

When they got home, she removed the tags from the clothing, washed the new items and tucked them into drawers the next morning. She hung the two dresses in the closet, next to Gracie's things. She wouldn't draw attention to them, hoping Hannah got used to seeing them.

Then she called Sevierville County Human Services for contact information for Hannah's former foster mother. "I'm hoping to gain insight into Hannah's emotions. Her triggers," she explained to the social worker who'd brought Hannah to Carly's several weeks before. "Avoiding meltdowns would be a step in the right direction."

"Ms. Bradley, you know we can't give out personal information without written permission, and I don't have that," Mrs. Wilkins replied. "If I don't reach her, I'll leave her a message."

Carly thanked her and hung up. Getting accurate information about kids in the system was often a struggle. It would be so much easier if parents could talk frankly, without having to go through Human Services.

Suddenly she had a thought.

She went to social media.

There were a few foster parent blogs and podcasts, and groups situated in various parts of the country, but nothing in their area. In twenty minutes she'd set up an Eastern Tennessee Foster Parents' page and put it out there.

By ten o'clock that night, they had nearly a hundred members. Not huge by internet standards, but large enough to offer advice and support.

They wouldn't share vulnerable information or pictures of kids. She made that clear. But if an experienced teacher was befuddled by children's behavior, were others experiencing the same thing? And could they help one another?

She hoped so.

Chapter Ten

Mike was pretty sure half the sheriff's department disliked him. That made rough odds to assume command in the fall.

"I wish I could disagree, but I can't," Sheriff Byrne told him when Mike broached the subject on Friday morning. The sheriff's expression reflected the concern in his voice. "Maybe bringing you in on a temporary basis wasn't a smart idea. I blame Coach," he added wryly. "I can say that now that he's doing better."

Coach Wynn was regaining strength, but he had a long road of recovery ahead of him and wouldn't resume coaching anytime soon.

"If his heart had behaved, you wouldn't be coaching and we'd be on even ground, but no one in this town goes against Wynn's wishes," Byrne continued. "The man's won too many games and healed too many hearts for us to be foolish about that. He picked you because he could trust you to do it right. His words, not mine," he added when Mike quirked his brow in question. "That move is making others angry. Sometimes that's just how it goes."

"The town puts a mighty high value on winning," noted Mike. "I like winning, but my goal is to see kids learn and grow. If they do that, the score generally takes care of itself. No one wins all the time," he finished.

"We hadn't lost to the Tigers in seven years," Byrne replied. "A couple of our guys took it personally because they've got kids on the team. Too personally, according to Coach Wynn. Enough so the best interests of the kids are being kicked to the curb. Wynn balanced both. He taught the ability to win by inspiration. Not everyone coaching kids has that skill."

His words underscored some of the behaviors Mike had called out during practices. Were the boys quietly being taught how to cheat the system? Fool the refs?

"I'd like your thoughts on working here, Mike. What you're thinking now that you've been here awhile. Do you intend to accept the sheriff's job?" Byrne asked frankly. "Or are you heading back to Nashville when your three months are up?"

A moment of truth had arrived. "I love it here." The honesty of the words surprised Mike. "You don't realize there's no peace and quiet in the city until you come to where you're surrounded by peace and quiet. The area is great. Kendrick Creek and its people are amazing. They've made me feel welcome," he told the sheriff. "The only place that feels awkward is right here, and with some of the team stuff that's going on." He stood. So did the sheriff. "I don't like making waves for no reason. Ruffling feathers for the good of the department is fine on occasion. That's what happens when you're in charge, but this infighting about football and the force isn't good. One shouldn't affect the other."

"Want me to step in?" the sheriff asked.

That was the last thing Mike wanted. "That would only fuel the fire. Let's give it a little more time," he said as he moved toward the door. "The town likes winning, but they also know Isaiah is injured, so maybe the timing is justified. Maybe the town's meant to be a little more realistic about the goals of a game."

"Oh, they're realistic, Mike." The sheriff shot Mike a meaningful look. "Winning *is* the goal. Coach was able to do that and develop healthy hearts and mindsets, so you've got big footsteps to fill. There." He motioned outside. "And here. Let me know if you need my help."

"I will, sir. And thanks for the advice. I think."

The sheriff didn't laugh, but he did give Mike a friendly clap on the back. "Football is separate from the job, but the town is entwined with it. Parents, kids, grandparents, business owners. It's not like a big city. There are no lines of separation here. It's just a matter of where and how often those lines intersect."

Those wise words gave him something to think about for about ten minutes, right up until two of his colleagues turned their backs on him as he walked by. A turned back was a sign of disrespect.

He could say something.

He chose not to.

Leadership didn't ride on words. It grew on deeds, and his goal was to do the job the best he could every single day. And if these guys regretted their treatment of him later, that was on them. He didn't hold grudges. His parents had taught him better than that.

But he did have a long memory, and mistreating a

colleague for perceived offenses was unacceptable if it continued.

One of the detectives called him over. He crossed the floor. The detective held up a picture of Orrie in his car, once again parked in an area where his only choice would be to back out. "I knew you were there that night, I read your report, and we advised the owner of the vehicle and his wife that he was liable. But here he is, two weeks later, doing the same thing with that old car he bought while his son was at war in Iraq." He indicated the big pink car. "Orrie said he wanted Teddy to come back to something special. Only Teddy never got the chance. It was a tough loss on his dad. One he's never really gotten over."

Anger didn't just creep up Mike's spine. It raced. The old man had seemed penitent the night he'd backed into Isaiah. He could have killed two kids. Kids Mike was coming to love. He choked back emotion as he faced the detective. "I'll go straight over. Are we ready to take his license?"

"We're ready to unregister the car. He's got another car to drive that has no visibility issues. His wife drives it all the time. Roche lives up the road from them, he says she's got it all together, but Orrie is stubborn."

Roche was another deputy. His boy played on Isaac's team.

"I'll go around there now." Mike took the address. "He could have killed those kids."

"More importantly, he took out our first-string quarterback," offered another detective. He saw Mike's horrified reaction and frowned. "Morris. I'm kidding. Did you leave your sense of humor back in Nashville?" he quipped. "Because we sure don't see any trace of it around here."

He refused to respond because injured kids were no laughing matter, but as he drove his SUV cruiser to Orrie's place, the truth broadsided him.

He didn't have a sense of humor anymore. He didn't joke around with the guys about anything. He barely opened his mouth, and when he did, it was almost condescending.

You've become a jerk.

He called Sean and when his brother answered, he asked him straight-out. "Am I a jerk?"

Sean answered so fast that it seemed like he'd been waiting for the question. "I prefer to call it a long dry spell of no laughter, Mike. And you've got a lot of hot-button topics that either make you angry or earn folks a lecture. So no, you're not a jerk. You're just acting like one."

Mike swallowed a lump of anger and redirected his question. "Nothing's fun, Sean. Or funny."

"Because you're angry and feel short-changed and you want to take it out on someone, but there's no one to pummel when we lose someone we love. And it's worse to lose two. But maybe it's more than that, little brother."

Mike wasn't sure how there could be more than that. "I'm listening."

"Listen, I'm not a therapist, and you stubbornly refused to go talk to anyone about this—"

"And still have no intention of doing so," Mike cut in.

"Which leads us right back to the stubborn Morris mentality," Sean continued. "But I think if you were standing outside the situation, you'd see what I see. What a bunch of us see," he added.

"You're mad at what happened. You're mad at God for letting them die or taking them. But I think you're mostly mad at Hallie."

Sean's words sliced deep.

"You're angry that she didn't make sure the doctor understood her condition fully. If she'd spoken up like she had multiple times before, told them about her anorexia as a teen and young adult, they might have red-flagged the heart issues that go along with that."

"She shouldn't have had to say anything. It was part of her medical history," barked Mike, and he didn't apologize for the strength of his tone.

"Except that doctors don't always have time to read fifteen or twenty years of records."

Emotion thrummed up Mike's spine so quick that his neck hurt. "You're blaming Hallie for this?"

"I'm not." Sean's voice went soft. "But I think you are."

Mike hung up.

His hands shook. His heart rate jumped. He pulled over, parked the cruiser and got out. A creek ran adjacent to the road here, one of those picturesque winding creeks that tumbled its way out of the Smokies down to the valley below.

He fisted his hands. Hauled in a breath. And then, for just a moment, he didn't even want to breathe. He wanted to be done with the anger, the pain, the solitude, the lack of joy. All of it.

He just wanted to be happy again. To not feel guilty and alone and bereft. To feel human.

Like you do at Carly's. With her. With those kids. But

one little conversation with your brother and you're
flying off the handle. Not good, man. Not good at all.

The mental warning was right, but how could he fix
this? How did one step from one life into another without guilt and sorrow?

He got back into his cruiser. As he drove through
Kendrick Creek, he turned toward the county line. The
church stood to his right, and the pastor, a youngish but
already balding man was there, watering the flowers.

Mike pulled in. He parked the cruiser, crossed the dry,
sad-looking grass and met the pastor on the sidewalk.

"Good morning, Deputy." The pastor wiped his hand
on the side of his pants and stuck it out. "I'm Bob Ja-
cobs. You're the new football coach, aren't you?"

Mike nodded. He accepted the hand. Then he shoved
his hands into his pockets because he wasn't sure what
else to do with them. "I'm not here about football."

"All right." The pastor set the hose down. "Do you
want to talk inside?"

"I don't want to talk."

The pastor waited.

"I want to feel better. I want to wake up and not
feel like punching God in the face, and that's a trick
because I don't even believe in Him, not the way everyone around me seems to, and yet, if I don't believe
in Him, why am I so angry? How can you be angry at
something that doesn't exist?" he demanded.

The pastor didn't seem surprised by Mike's stand.
"You've got an age-old question with no answers because, if God doesn't exist, why would we get emotional
talking about Him? What spurs us to anger? And if He

does exist, why is our world filled with strife and anger and loss and grief?"

"Yes. It makes no sense."

"But, of course, it *does* make sense," the pastor countered. "God gave us free will and left us to either follow His word, to believe and live our lives in a humble way, or to reject the whole idea and do what we please. Being in law enforcement, you know that doesn't work so well. That's why we have laws."

"Laws offer the basic structure a society needs."

"Exactly," agreed the pastor. "Sports have rules, too. And expectations. Maybe those are more appropriately called guidelines. But even with those rules, you need referees or umpires to call the games correctly because not everyone plays fair."

"Rules give athletes the information they need about their position, the game, the play."

"Faith isn't all that different. We play by the basic rules we were given a long time ago. We question. We forge ahead. And if we're blessed with the gift of faith, it's that much easier."

"And if you don't want the gift? If it's inconsequential?" Mike asked.

"Then you have to ask yourself why you pulled in here. Why something that matters so little is troubling you."

When Mike was about to react, the pastor raised a hand.

"You don't have to respond, Coach. We're just throwing things out there. It's a rugged world. Good stuff and bad stuff happens every day. Faith can strengthen us to hold strong in the hard times, but hard times are part of the equation."

Mike swiveled and walked away. The pastor turned the hose back on, gently watering the mulched ground beneath the flowers. Mike climbed into the cruiser, turned it around and then paused. He rolled down the window.

The pastor looked up and stopped watering.

Mike frowned. He looked at the pastor, then the flowers, then the sky. He took a deep breath and offered the pastor a silent salute, two fingers to the brim of his cap.

The pastor did the same. Then he went back to watering the garden.

Mike drove on to Orrie's house. He pulled into the driveway and parked. The infamous big pink car was parked by an old garage out back.

Move forward...

He wanted to. But how?

Same as you did when you were a new cop on the beat. One step at a time.

The first step had been coming here. Changing things up. And now he was going to take the second step. He sent Carly a quick text. Bonfire at my house after practice. You. Me. Kids. Smoky dogs on the grill. Sound good?

He waited in the driveway, wanting one simple answer. When he got it, he smiled. Sounds wonderful.

Could supper with four kids be considered a date?

Not under normal circumstances, Carly decided, but her life wasn't exactly normal and the idea of a family date sounded pretty nice.

She took Gracie to the store to grab some things

they'd need for true Eastern Tennessee hot dogs. Things Mike might not know. Cabbage for coleslaw. A can of chili. Cheese. And a box of pasta for macaroni salad.

A call from Sean came in as she tucked Gracie's seat into place when she was done shopping. "Hey, Sean."

"Are you home?"

"Nope. I'm in the grocery store parking lot. With kids. About to head home. What's going on?"

"Lida Gables wants to see Gracie."

Her heart stopped because the thought of a face-to-face with Lida could be wonderful or a recipe for disaster. "Is that allowed?"

"It shouldn't be," Sean replied. "We're involved in a litigation and there shouldn't be contact between the two of you because anything that happens can be used in the petition. That could affect Gracie's future."

"So who's advising her to do this, Sean?"

"I asked her that very question, Carly," he answered softly. "I don't think anyone is. I think she just wants to see her baby."

What mother wouldn't? And how cruel was Carly to want to block this action? "I don't know what to do."

"Say no for now and let the legal process work," he advised. "If the judge sides with Lida, she'll see Grace soon enough."

"But if I talk to her—"

"And convince her to drop the petition and then she uses that against you?" Sean clicked his tongue like he'd done before. "I know this is hard, but I'm advising against communication. We're not talking a normal conversation between two women here. We're talking a face-to-face between opposite sides of a custody battle.

You hired me to be straight with you, Carly. Seeing Lida would be a bad thing to do at this juncture."

She hated this. She hated fighting the kids' mother, fighting for her right to keep Gracie when Lida had given birth to her, but Lida had given birth to all four children. You couldn't just select which one you wanted to love. You should love them all. "Go with your gut, Sean. I trust you."

"Good."

The decision plagued her all the way home. Guilt set in because Lida's overture meant Carly wasn't just a faceless person in a lawsuit right now. She was the person blocking a mother from seeing her child, and that felt wrong. So wrong. But what could she do?

She tucked the baby in for her afternoon nap when she got tired and put the salad in the fridge. Then she sat and wrote Lida Gables a letter.

She printed it, folded it and put it into an envelope. She put Lida's name on the envelope, but she didn't mail it. Not yet.

She slipped the envelope into a high cupboard where the boys wouldn't see it.

Prayer. Thoughts. And more prayer. Those were the essentials before she did anything else. Sean was right; a visit or a letter could tip the decision against Carly.

She didn't want that.

She wanted Gracie to stay and so she'd written her heart out onto a page, but she was going to wait until the time was right to send it.

How would she know that?

By putting trust in God.

Chapter Eleven

Hannah raced for the driveway the moment Mike's SUV pulled in to pick up the boys for practice later that afternoon. She leapt into his arms, clung tight and buried her sweet face in the big deputy's neck. For a moment, Carly wished she had the sweet abandon to do the exact same thing.

She didn't.

Mike planted a kiss to Hannah's forehead and snugged her along his left hip as if she belonged there.

"Did you need the boys to be ready early?" asked Carly. "Because getting things done on time is tricky enough."

He smiled, but there was a serious look behind the smile. "No." He spoke softly, and she drew closer to hear. Close enough for that scent to waft over her again. Clean. Fresh. Mountain-woods friendly. "I wanted a quick minute with you before we head to town. I installed a wheel lock on Orrie Sims's car this morning."

"You locked the car?"

"We had a video of him parking where he'd need to

back up again. A store manager turned him in because he heard what happened at the park two weeks ago."

"I can't believe he drove it again, knowing what he'd done." Orrie wasn't an awful person. He was a tactless man, but he wasn't cruel. He knew better. "That's heartless."

"It was a foolish thing to do for a lot of reasons. I felt bad for him when I realized what the car meant to him," he admitted. "But it's done. Like it should be."

He'd done what he needed to do even though it had been hard. He could have sent someone else to do it. But he hadn't. "I don't know what to say except thank you. That's what town heroes do, Mike. They look out for others."

"No hero here, Carly." His face shadowed. Then it smoothed. "Orrie was holding on to a past that disappeared. But it's taken care of now." He released a breath that was almost a sigh. Then he redirected his attention to the little girl in his arms. "Hey, princess. How was your day? Did you have fun?"

Hannah didn't answer him. She simply held on tight, and when he set her down to take the boys to practice, her sad expression wrenched Carly's heart. She clearly loved Mike. Yearned for him.

Would she ever bond with Carly?

Reason said yes, but waiting it out was tough. Hannah ignored her older brothers, avoided Gracie most of the time and pretended Carly didn't exist. She only came to life around Mike. Did he remind her of someone? Or was he her port in the storm of life?

"So what do I need for tonight besides great sausages and nice, chewy rolls?" asked Mike as the boys came their way from the garage.

"Coleslaw and macaroni salad. Chili. Mustard, ketchup. Sweet onions."

"I've got the last three," he told her. I'll swing by the market and grab the other stuff on the way back tonight."

"No need. We're all set. I've got it."

His look of surprise made her smile. "I made a macaroni salad and coleslaw," she told him. "You've got the rest. We'll put together real Smoky Dogs when you get home. Isaiah will love it. Isaac will eat one or two plain hot dogs. And Hannah will be happy with ham and cheese, her daily ration of food."

"Thank you." He smiled down at her then didn't stop smiling, even as the boys reached the SUV. He locked eyes with her and when he raised his hand to her cheek, her pulse spiked. "See you in a couple of hours. And I've got the fire ready to light so we won't need to mess around with it later."

"Pretty nice, Mike."

His smile deepened and, for just a moment, she wondered what it would be like to lean forward. Let her lips touch his briefly.

"Coach, if we're late cuz of you, do we still have to run laps?" Isaac asked, and his question was enough to have Mike draw back.

"No, but I would have to, so let's get going. See you later, ladies." He waved out the window once he backed up.

Carly waved back.

So did Hannah.

And she sent a wistful look toward the road long seconds after Mike and the boys were out of sight.

Carly bent low. "We'll go over to Mike's house later,

okay? When he's home with your big brothers? And we can make a fire and roast marshmallows. All right?"

"My Mike?" Hannah pointed across the street. "Mine?"

Carly gave her a hug.

Hannah didn't want it. She stiffened right away, but Carly wasn't about to be dissuaded, and when Mike pulled in with the boys over two hours later, Hannah was thrilled.

They roasted hot dogs.

They told old Smoky Mountain stories, some that Carly remembered and a few Mike had learned from his parents. And when Hannah started falling asleep in Mike's arms, Carly rose. "Time to go."

"I know." Mike stood, balancing the sleepy four-year-old while Carly carried Gracie down the sloping driveway. He fell into step beside her. "This was nice, Carly. Real nice."

"It was." She slanted a smile up at him. A smile meant for him. "It was a great idea."

"I have another idea," he continued as they moved up the driveway. The boys were still roasting marshmallows at the fire. "My brother was wondering if we'd all like to come swimming tomorrow. They've got a pool and it might be a nice respite for the kids. I told him I'd check with you, but I don't want Isaiah to feel badly because he can't swim with the others."

"Broken bones and summer are a bad combination for sure," she agreed, but there was more to consider with Mike's offer. Tonight had been perfect. Just them, being themselves, sitting around a fire, laughing and talking.

Taking the kids to a family home with Mike was too much like a date to be considered anything else.

She didn't date. Hadn't dated in ages. And she had no intention of starting, so why was she so tempted?

Because of him.

The gray eyes. Wavy hair. The strength and warmth of a good man. Regardless, she refused the offer gently. "Isaiah is already giving up enough. To sit and watch all the kids have fun in the pool would be tough. I think we'll just lay low. Sunday will be busy with football and then school starts on Monday. That's a whole new season for the kids to deal with."

"Will you miss going back this semester?" he asked as she got Gracie ready for bed. He was still holding Hannah. She'd curled into his arms and yawned. Her quiet eyes looked sleepy.

"Yes and no." She slipped a baby nightshirt over Gracie's head and lifted her off the changing table. "I love my job. But I'm glad to have these months to get life settled here. And glad I rarely needed sick time because having those extra days is huge. It will be weird to stay home on Monday. But right now I want every day I can get with Gracie and I want Miss Hannah to trust me." She smiled into the little girl's eyes. She tucked Gracie in then came back for Hannah.

"Stay." Hannah clung to Mike's neck, refusing to let go.

"I can't, honey. I have to go home." Mike tried to unwind her arms from his neck.

"Stay. Stay. Stay."

"I'll see you tomorrow. I promise," he told her. Carly helped unwind Hannah's entwined fingers from his neck.

Mike stepped back.

Hannah cried. Sad tears, not big, in-your-face tears.

That same grief they'd witnessed in the clothing store swept over her. "Just stay. Just stay."

Carly's heart went tight.

She was a great teacher. She knew that. She had the awards, accolades and successes to prove it. But how did one become a great mother? How would you even know if what you were doing or choosing was right? She had no idea. Seeing her soon-to-be adopted daughter break down, she was pretty sure everything she was doing was wrong.

Mike wisely made a quick escape. "See you tomorrow, princess." He slipped out the door. Carly locked the screen and then closed and locked the inside door as well, just in case Hannah decided to track her hero down in the dark.

Then she settled into the rocker with Hannah.

The cool air of the AC added a level of comfort. Hannah cried softly for a few minutes then dozed off. When Carly tucked her into bed, she stood for a moment, watching the girls. Her girls. She wasn't picking or choosing who to raise or what to do. She'd purposely gone in for the long haul.

Jordan had shared sage words not long ago. Let go. Let God.

It wasn't as simple as the words made it sound. She understood that. But she'd taken a leap of faith when she'd said yes to the girls. It was time to take another one now.

Chapter Twelve

Mike could have spent Saturday at Sean's house, grilling burgers and lounging by the pool with his nephew and nieces. It was a real temptation, but he stayed home instead and cleaned out the garage.

You're officially old, his brother texted. Guys who spend Saturdays cleaning a garage are past prime. Just so you know.

Not old. Time-sensitive, Mike shot back. Or just plain smart.

Sticking with old. Coming to game tomorrow. Figured there'd be five people on the bleachers that like you.

An unfortunate yet accurate assessment. See you then.

Mike got about halfway through the job when a noise overhead drew his attention.

He looked up.

Twin eyes gazed back at him from the dark loft.

His heart leapt. His hand went straight to his waist. He pulled his weapon.

Another set of eyes joined the first. Then another. A tiny sound came from the shadows. A soft mew.

Kittens.

He stowed the gun and eyed the loft. How had the mother gotten up there? And where was she?

These babies were small. Not yet feral, but if he didn't get them used to people soon, they would be. And the lofted storage area meant a possible long drop to the concrete floor below. He set up a ladder, climbed up and crawled into the loft. There were several old trunks in the far back corner that had been overlooked or ignored for the estate sale. The garage light was below the loft, leaving the loft dark except for his flashlight.

He texted Carly. Kittens in loft. Assistance required. Don't want them to fall. Me, either.

Within minutes, she was there with a small cage-type thing and the entourage.

Isaac scrambled up the ladder like a champion.

Gracie was in the stroller and Hannah clapped her hands in glee the moment she spotted Mike up above.

"How many are there?" asked Carly. "Do you need help?"

Isaac didn't wait for Mike to answer. "I see three, Mom, and maybe there's a number four in the corner."

"There is definitely movement in the corner," reported Mike as he aimed his flashlight that way. "Not sure if it's friend or foe."

"And never good to assume anything in the country," Carly reminded him. "Go get 'em, and we'll tuck them into our version of a secure facility."

"Got one!" Isaac handed off a fluff-ball orange kitten to Mike. Mike reached down.

Carly reached up. A narrow distance prevented the handoff, so she climbed the first two rungs of the ladder.

She smelled good. Like summertime and fresh air and coconut sunscreen. He handed her the first kitten, and her face went soft. "Hey, baby. Hey. We've got you. Come on down and meet the family."

"Careful on that ladder," he told her then wasn't sure why he'd said it. The ladder was fine. She was fine.

She looked up again, smiling, and he knew. Right there, in that moment, he knew why he'd cautioned her about the ladder. Why last evening had felt so right and why he'd stayed home when she'd refused the offer to go swimming.

He was falling for her.

It wasn't exactly a shock because Carly Bradley was everything a smart man wanted. He'd already figured that out. No, the amazing part was that he'd been sure he'd never have those feelings again. He'd have sworn to it, but he'd have been wrong because, meeting her gaze, he knew he was falling. And it felt good.

Isaac had caught the second kitten, a smoke-gray baby, not as long-haired. He handed it off to Mike. Mike stooped low, leaned over and handed the kitten down to Carly.

She settled her hands around his to receive the kitten.

He slipped one hand out and clasped it over hers, squeezing lightly to test her reaction.

She smiled up. He smiled down and, for a long moment, he wasn't thinking about kittens.

"Got the third one!" Excitement hiked Isaac's voice.

"You're good at this, kid." He winked at Carly then backed up into the loft again. "Really good. So what do we think's in that back corner?"

"Do not try to catch a raccoon, rat, mouse or whatever might be lurking in the shadows," ordered Carly from below. "No one has time for an ER visit today."

"Whatever it is, it's dark," reported Isaac a few seconds later. "So I—" His voice broke. He scrambled into the corner. His efforts blocked the beam from Mike's flashlight. The hardware store variety didn't light up a room like the one on his service revolver, but when Isaac turned, Mike grinned. "Kitten number four rescue complete!"

"Mom, this is the cutest one of all." Isaac came to the side, handed a black-based calico kitten off to Mike and then grinned down at his mother. "She's got all the colors!"

"I love calicos," breathed Carly. "Hey, kitty, let's get you in the crate with your brothers and sister, okay? No sign of mom?" she asked Mike.

He shook his head. "No. And they seem hungry."

"If we leave them outside in the shade, she'll come around if she's able."

Mike knew what she meant. Life as a roaming cat in the mountains came with risk. "And if she's not?"

"The farm stores will have a milk replacement. I think the kittens are about three weeks old. Eyes open, just able to walk and not turned off by humans yet."

Hannah had been watching Mike.

Isaac came down the ladder quickly. Mike followed. Hannah staked her claim instantly and jumped into his arms. Her neediness called to the protector in him. But then Gracie looked up.

His heart tightened. Or maybe it was his gut. He wasn't sure, but every time he looked into Gracie's sweet face, he pictured Wyatt. What would his son be like now? What would he sound like? Act like?

Would he look like Mike's baby pictures? Or Hallie's?

It wasn't fair for Gracie to live with constant comparisons, and how could he get beyond the crushing weight of that?

"Meow!" Hannah clapped her hands as she mewed to her new little friends. They were setting up a loud chorus to protest their new living arrangements and Hannah echoed them with an expression of pure joy. "Meow!" she said again and laughed out loud. "Meow! Meow!"

"You like the kittens?" Mike stooped low so she could see them better.

Hannah's face transformed. Worry was wiped away. Sheer delight had taken its place. Transfixed, she watched the kittens prowl around in the small crate, looking for a way out.

"While these guys are adorable, my practical side says we need a litter box and milk replacer ASAP," Carly told them. "Isaiah, do you want to come with me to get them? Or stay here?"

"I'll stay and help Coach," he said. "If that's all right, Mom?"

"I'll go because I know 'zactly what to get in that store," announced Isaac.

"Hannah, let's go to the store and get some things for Coach, okay?"

The look on Hannah's face spoke volumes. She kept her arms firmly around Mike's neck. "Stay."

"She's fine," Mike told Carly. "Unless you want me to run and get the stuff. Or we could all go," he suggested.

"I don't know if Farmer's Supply needs the whole dog and pony show," said Carly. "Is this crate big enough for a small litter box for our little friends?"

"Just."

"Mom, we have a bigger one in the space over our garage," said Isaiah. "Will it bother Barney if we bring the kittens over there?"

"We should leave them as close to where we found them as possible," replied Carly, "but I forgot about that old kennel. That would be the perfect size, Isaiah."

"Divide and conquer." Mike made the suggestion sound normal. It was anything but. He wanted her to feel secure about leaving Isaiah and Hannah, but he had to steel himself to avoid going one-on-one with the baby.

It was his problem. Not hers. Yet since he didn't know how to fix it, the problem remained. "You take two. I keep two."

"Fair enough. We'll be back soon. Hit the bathroom, bud." Carly hooked a thumb toward her house as she addressed Isaac. "Before we head out."

"I will, Mom!" Isaac hurried across the street. Carly followed, pushing Gracie in the stroller, while Mike stayed with Hannah and Isaiah.

He crossed the road with the two kids once Carly had left and procured the pieces of dog crate from the storage area above Carly's garage. They assembled the bigger kennel in the shadow of the oak tree that shaded the front of Mike's house. Mike set it up on his porch, grabbed a pop for him and Isaiah, poured apple juice for Hannah, and toasted their success. "We did it."

Isaiah laughed at him. "It's only five pieces, Coach. With the floor missing and all."

"Don't minimize the effort, son." Mike bumped his bottle to Isaiah's. "A real man learns to never minimize effort."

Except hadn't he done just that by sending Gracie off with Carly? He'd taken the easy path. He'd avoided babies for over two years for good reason. But how was he going to handle that now? Because Gracie deserved more than casual regard or a distant friend.

She required the best he could give.

Only, Mike wasn't sure he had it in him.

A good share of the town showed up for Sunday's football game, even with the heat index in the high 90s. They brought folding chairs and sat them in the shade of nearby trees. Some brought pop-up tents to offer respite from the sun, but as the game heated up, most folks got out of their chairs and paced the sidelines.

Hannah wanted to see Mike, so Carly took a spot on the bleachers. The girls wore sun hats, Isaiah was stressed about being sidelined, and Isaac was having lunch with a teammate after they'd won the earlier game.

A small group of football mothers huddled nearby. Mike was the topic of their disgruntled discussion. Did they know he was her neighbor? Did they know she and Isaiah could hear every word? Did they care?

She had Gracie on her lap. Hannah was studying a picture book with great intensity. Isaiah was next to her, alongside the bleacher. He wasn't sitting. He was standing with the aid of a crutch, watching the team lineup. "I hate being part of the crowd." Isaiah muttered the words softly.

"I know. Hopefully by September you'll be back."

"And then I have to get practices in before I'm eligible."

"It's for your safety, son."

Isaiah wasn't impressed. He indicated the grumpy women with a sideways glance. "Are folks always like this?"

"Some. There was less grumbling with Coach Wynn, but still a fair share. Everyone's got an opinion."

"I'm going to stand with the team."

She nodded. She'd move, too, but Hannah had picked this spot and Carly wasn't about to upset her.

She didn't have to be there. Isaiah wasn't playing and she could have simply dropped him off and stayed home with the girls, but team support was important and getting Hannah out and about with people was crucial. She had no idea how the first day of school would go, but assimilating Hannah into the community was part of Carly's job.

"There's no reason not to run Beck today," whispered one woman. Beck Benson was a strong player. His parents had split up two years before and had been quarreling ever since. Beck's mother had summer custody and took him north to a sports camp. The camp polished skill levels, but league rules said every athlete had to put in a set number of team practices to be eligible to play in games. "He's been in camp, not sitting home surrounded by screens. His mother's selfishness isn't the kid's fault. So who's this guy going to put in? The girl?" Disbelief colored her tone. "There's a sound choice."

"Beck looks so sad," replied one of the other women.

"Wynn would have played him." It was the third woman talking. The certainty in her assertion was wrong.

Wynn wouldn't have, not without the required practices, although Coach Wynn was known to provide kids with extra practice opportunities to get things done properly. But then, Wynn was retired. He didn't have a full-time job limiting his coaching time.

"This guy might be easy on the eyes, but he's a rule-follower. Everyone knows you don't win games by following the rules. Not all of them, anyhow."

Carly wanted to speak up.

She didn't. She might have their kids in her class when she went back to work in January, and she didn't want football issues to mess with classroom dynamics. Still, she couldn't shut them out, and she didn't want to upset Hannah's peace by moving, so she tried to ignore them. It was an impossible task.

"Jed says he can be a jerk at work."

Jed Kennedy was a sheriff's deputy, and his son had just moved up a team level after a massive spring growth spurt. Jed's wife, Crystal, loved to talk.

"He rubs some of the guys the wrong way," she went on, "but Jed told them to pipe down."

"Why?"

"Because the guy lost his wife and baby a couple of years back and he's been sad ever since. Jed heard it from a friend who works with the coach's brother in Newport."

Mike lost his wife and baby?

Carly's gut clenched. He'd never said a word. She had no idea, and she'd been his neighbor for weeks.

"Well, why doesn't anyone know this stuff?" huffed another woman.

"Maybe because we shouldn't have to know someone's personal business to be kind?" It was the fourth woman. She'd been quiet up to that point. "Maybe being nice should come first."

"You are right about that, Zoey." It was Jed Kennedy's wife talking. "Now I'm embarrassed, because I know better."

"I know better, too," shot back the first one. "But he's gonna lose this game because he doesn't have a first string QB and he won't bend the rules, so we'll end up with a third-string quarterback for the first game of the season after he messes up this scrimmage. The Northern Tennessee Tigers are going to eat us up and spit us out. Mark my words."

Hannah looked up at Carly then. She pointed to the playground.

"You want to go play?"

Hannah nodded.

"Let's do it." She took the girls to the playground and spent nearly half the game entertaining Gracie while Hannah played alone, surrounded by a cluster of noisy kids. Watching Hannah gave her time to contemplate what she'd just heard.

Mike had lost his wife and his child.

She couldn't imagine that pain. The physical, mental and emotional drain. It explained the shadow in his eyes. The lost look she'd seen. A look he'd quickly masked, which meant he'd been masking it for a while. How utterly, awfully, heartbreaking.

When she brought the girls back to their spot on the bleachers, three big cookies sat on top of her hamper. She frowned, puzzled.

Isaiah held one up. "Coach."

"How nice. What's the score?"

"Twelve to twelve."

"Low score for three quarters."

"Yeah." He frowned at his casted leg. "Longest August ever."

"School will make it go by quickly," she told him.

He gave her a funny look. "Oddly that's not as comforting as you hoped it would be."

She laughed, broke a cookie in two and offered it to Hannah. "From Coach Mike. A present for you."

"Mike!" Hannah had no trouble getting excited about the big guy. She scrambled onto the bleachers and scanned the spread-out crowd. "Mike!" she called, looking for him. "Mike!"

"He's over there, but he's busy, honey." Carly tried to distract her with the cookie. "You'll see him later."

A couple of the women exchanged looks but stayed quiet.

Hannah wasn't easily dissuaded. "Mike!" She hollered his name, hoping to be heard. Then she spotted him, up the line. She scrambled down the bleachers and raced his way.

Gracie was sleepy. She had her pacifier and was cozied up in Carly's arms. Isaiah had moved in the opposite direction, offering advice to the sideline players.

"How can I help?" One of the women sat next to Carly. "How about I take this one and you can corral the other?"

Gracie burst into tears. Normally amenable, she didn't like having her nap times rearranged and she wasn't big on strangers right now. "I'll send Isaiah down to get Hannah. That might avoid the meltdown. But thank you."

"Might be too late," drawled another mother. "I think Coach has done gone and gotten himself a lady friend."

Carly looked up.

There was Mike, still down near midfield, holding Hannah in his arms as he coached.

Isaiah saw what had happened and moved that way, but Mike seemed totally unconcerned about the four-year-old in his arms. He barked orders, gave directions and even threw his free hand into the air a couple of times.

Hannah didn't care.

Neither did the crowd. They seemed to like this softer side of their coach and when she finally released her hold on him when the fourth quarter was almost done, she hurried back to Carly's spot on the bleachers with one thing in mind. "Cookie? Please?"

She didn't point.

She didn't pout.

She'd said "please."

Carly gave her the cookie quickly. "There you go. Did you have a nice visit with Mike?"

"My Mike."

Staff development workshops taught about discouraging unrealistic dreams and goals for children, and Carly'd had her share of those over the years. But if this awkward, sad child wanted to call him "My Mike," Carly wasn't about to argue. "You saw the game? And the players?"

Hannah bit into the cookie and nodded. Then she pointed in Mike's direction. "My Mike loud." She made a face then smiled as if loud coaches were funny. "So loud!" She covered her ears but smiled harder, as if teasing.

Gracie had fallen asleep.

Hobbling on his crutches, Isaiah was upfield with the team, shouting encouragement. No one was there to witness Hannah's first bits of conversation with Carly. Then the other mother shifted her gaze from Hannah to Carly. "Your expression says this is a breakthrough."

"Huge."

"I work with Northeastern Mental Health," she said softly. "I'm a therapist there, but we live here in Kendrick Creek. I saw her affect, and reactions. And then yours. That's a marvelous feeling."

Hannah was busily eating the cookie, but she climbed to the back bleachers again so she could watch her hero as he coached the team to a twenty-to-twelve loss a few minutes later.

Parents grumbled. About fifty percent were certain they could have done a better job and produced a win. The other fifty percent were lamenting Coach Wynn's collapse, his choice in new coach and his lack of speed in getting well.

Mike seemed to ignore it all. He convened with the

players, reminded them about Tuesday's practice and the upcoming fundraiser, then sent them on their way.

A line of folks waited to talk to him. It wasn't a happy line. He'd only managed to get through four of them while she herded the kids to the car.

He was listening to them. He seemed to take their thoughts and complaints seriously. He even appeared to be considering their opinions, jotting things down into a notebook.

When she got home with the kids, a group text came in. Mike was calling a coaches' and parents' meeting for Monday night.

Would people come?

Yes.

She was fortunate to get a fifty percent response ratio for the school's annual fall open house, but people would come out for football. They always did.

The first night of school was a rough choice on Mike's part, but they'd come because Junior Volunteer parents didn't like losing and that made today a travesty in some minds. Not all—but a vocal few.

So they'd show up, if for no other reason than to let Mike know he was doing a terrible job. And she'd be there to let him know she felt just the opposite.

Chapter Thirteen

"I'm here. Hey, cuties." Jordan breezed through the front door just after five thirty Monday evening.

"Thank you." Carly slipped her phone into the side pocket of her purse. "Isaiah is upstairs. Isaac is sorting through the massive stack of papers the school feels required to dispense on day one. Gracie's teething—she's not happy about the situation and neither one of us has had much sleep." She leaned closer to Jordan to make her point. "She is not a stoic child."

"Oh, man. Sorry." Jordan made a face of regret. "You do look tired."

"For good reason. Can you imagine how tough this would be if I'd gone back to work this week? God bless working mothers everywhere," she whispered. Then louder, she added, "The meeting shouldn't be more than an hour, there's mac and cheese for supper and ham rolls in the fridge. I've got my phone. Call if you need me, okay?"

"I will, but we should be fine. How did Hannah handle the first day of school?"

Carly winced. "She doesn't start pre-K until Wednesday, but having the boys disappear this morning made her restless and unhappy. She stood guard half the day. Watching. Waiting. Hence the added security to the upper half of the doors," she said softly. "It made her sad to be here alone with me and Gracie."

Being home with no big brothers had clearly displeased the four-year-old. She'd kept folding her arms. Tapping her toe. Watching the door. The road. The yard. And when Carly had explained what was happening, Hannah had turned her back and walked away.

And then she'd snuck peeks out the front window as if willing the boys home. Eyeing the door. Weighing her prospects.

Carly had installed a higher lock on both doors. She pointed it out to Jordan nonverbally. If she drew attention to the device, Hannah would try to figure out how to open it. Better for all of them that she simply couldn't get the door open. With a big, busy family, it was far too easy to lose track of a little girl with escape on her mind.

"We've got this," Jordan assured her. "I make the best mac and cheese on the planet, and Isaiah will help me if needed."

"I can help, too," Isaac chimed in.

Carly called goodbye to Isaiah and kissed Isaac's forehead. "I'll see you later. Love you." She slipped out the side door. A moment later, she heard Jordan put the small upper lock in place.

She hurried down the drive, got into the car and drove to the town offices.

No one was there. A handwritten sign on the door said "Meeting moved to football field due to overcrowding."

Poor Mike.

He'd said he'd coached for years, but were Nashville-area parents as tough as their Eastern Tennessee counterparts? Carly had no way of knowing, but after teaching in the district for over twenty years, she knew how much Kendrick Creek loved sports, and especially football.

The bleachers were packed and people stood shoulder to shoulder to the left and right of the bleachers. All ten coaches were there. Most seemed fine, but a couple of Isaiah's coaches looked smug. Mike's back was to them, but Carly found their expressions worrisome.

Coach Wynn would have schmoozed the crowd a little. Offered a joke or two, some lighthearted banter, something to ease his way into the required annual coaches-parents talk on manners and behaviors. The league and the schools had mandated these talks over a decade ago when fan behavior had taken a downward turn.

Mike didn't use small talk or humor. He waded right in. If he noticed some of the parents bristling, he ignored it. He introduced the coaches, leaving himself for last.

Wynn would have given each coach a moment to introduce himself.

Not Mike.

He gave the standard intro written about each coach on the league web page, paused while parents cheered their favorite, and kept on going.

"I know it's the first day of school," Mike said. "And I don't want to keep you here long, but it's required that we meet, talk, answer questions before the first sanctioned league game on Sunday. With three nights of practice, this seemed like the best option.

"I want to stress that if any of the coaches hear derogatory remarks or inappropriate behaviors on either sideline, ours or the opposition's, those people will be escorted to their cars. There's no place for ugly rhetoric in youth sports."

He paused, deliberately. Scanned the crowd. "Some of you are angry that Coach Wynn asked me to step in, some are mad about how I conducted our opening scrimmage. I also hear some of you are riled about a girl on the team, about required practices, about the sun being in the sky and the trees making too much noise in the wind so you can't hear the calls properly. I don't care." He drew out the final three words while slowly scanning the audience. "I'm not here to placate your feelings, or to follow everything Coach Wynn did verbatim, or to smooth ruffled feathers of other coaches. That stuff means nothing to me. Know what does?" he asked outright. It was rhetorical and he continued after a brief pause.

"Your kids. Their skills, their emotions, the way they feel about themselves, the way they see a job well done and want to emulate it. They're my focus. They're my goal. Watching them grow into fine young men and women by understanding how a team works. By knowing that following rules is important. By learning that training outranks cheap tricks and cheating, and we all know there was a problem with that last season."

A few people exchanged sheepish looks. Expressions that showed they knew exactly what Mike was talking about.

Mike splayed his hands. "These kids are good athletes. Strong players. Strong teams. What I've seen shows me we've got a lot to work with, and if we're all on the same page, we can move forward together. If we're not, the Northern Tennessee Tigers are willing to file a formal protest that shows a history of unfair practices last year."

A ripple of unease went through the crowd. Not most of the crowd. Just some. But enough to know that Mike's words hit home.

"NTT is jealous," scoffed one of the dads. "They don't train like we do, run fast enough or work hard enough to win on their own dime so they want to ruin things for us. We don't give in to a bunch of city lovers. Not here."

Mike held the man's gaze. Then, slowly and deliberately, he turned his attention to a few of the fathers in the crowd. And then he glanced back at his coaches. Specifically the Under 13 group. "I've seen the video."

Two coaches winced.

"No one gets away with stuff these days," he said seriously. "Everyone's watching and half are filming. So the videos are out there, and if we clean up our act, they've agreed to let it drop. We play hard, clean and controlled. That's my mantra. And that's how I expect this season to go, from the first game on. And that's all I've got to say. Thank you for coming."

Parents exchanged glances.

Coach Wynn always offered a question-and-answer time after the mandated meeting.

Mike took the brief notes he'd never even looked at and walked toward his SUV.

Carly didn't stay to see the reactions in the crowd.

She drove home, pulled into her driveway, parked and walked across the road. Mike was on the porch, in one of the rockers, but he didn't look content. He looked resigned.

She climbed the steps and took a seat on the glider. It squeaked when she pushed it, a comforting sound. Like an old friend talking. "That went well."

He lifted one brow because they both understood the opposite truth.

"Has there been cheating going on?"

He nodded.

"Is that why Coach tagged you to take over the team?"

"Yes. He approached my brother when he learned I was moving here. Sean wasn't sure it was a good time. I hadn't coached since—" He gazed off, over the narrow road, over the trees, then worked his jaw. "Not since my wife and unborn son died."

"Oh, Mike." She reached out and laid her hand atop his. "I'm so sorry you had to go through that. No one should have to face a loss like that."

He looked at her. "You knew."

"Just recently. One of the mothers was talking about it and I overheard her. I figured if you wanted people to know, you'd tell them."

"An online search brings it right up. Hallie Jean Morris and unborn son Wyatt."

"Which means I haven't been online stalking you. Why do that when the real deal has moved in across the street?"

He tried to smile. It half worked. Then he sighed.

Her heart hurt for him. Not just for the loss, but for the ache in his eyes. His gaze. In him. "I can't even imagine that kind of pain, Mike. Just know that I'm sorry you had to go through it. So sorry."

The sorrow in her eyes said more than words.

He grimaced. "It's been awful. I came here *because*

it was awful. I didn't expect to get called into coaching. I'd said no to my brother. He'd filled me in on what was happening, and two of these guys are deputies. That makes it worse, if they have the mindset that getting away with something underhanded makes it all right. I didn't want to cloud the issue with colleagues, and Sean understood that, but when I got to that field and found the Coach barely breathing…" He sighed. "I couldn't say no."

"So you knew there was stuff going on?"

He braced his hands on the rocker's armrests. "Yes. But I needed to see it. Get a feel for it. And when I saw deliberate attempts at cheating and hurting the other team's players, I knew I had to address it. And so we had the meeting."

"Well, it was memorable, Mike."

He frowned because he knew there'd be fallout, but that was a by-product of cheating and misbehavior. Actions had consequences. "There're ways to do things right. That's an important thing to teach kids. How to excel at what they do. Not how to get away with things to make others fail."

"Those are admirable qualities, Mike. And a lot of folks are going to respect you for it."

"Some won't."

She shrugged. "Don't let the few negative people get to you. They love lauding it over the other teams in the region. Fairly childish." She stood. "I've got to get home. Tuck kids in. Snatch some sleep before Gracie's pain meds wear off and her teething kicks in again."

She looked tired. But still lovely. Not dolled-up lovely, either. Carly had a natural beauty that shone through long days and kids and antics and things going wrong. It called to him.

"Want help?"

She shook her head. "No, I've got this. Although offer again tomorrow night if tonight crashes and burns like last night did." She reached out and took his hand, and it didn't just feel good. It felt right. "You did well tonight. You cleared the air. I had no idea what was going on, so does that mean Isaiah didn't tell me? Or didn't know?"

"Your son doesn't need tricks to perform well. He's gifted, strong, and he practices all the time. Primarily it was a handful of kids whose fathers coached them how to play dirty and be fairly unseen by the refs."

"Shame on them."

He'd seen this kind of thing all through his foot-ball years. It wasn't new, but seeing it happening with twelve-year-old kids was an eye-opener. "Yes. But now we'll get it right. At least for this season. If Coach comes back and wants to coach again, he'll start with a clean slate. That's a good feeling."

She smiled up at him. "You're a good man, Mike Morris." She squeezed his hand lightly. "Good night."

He didn't let her hand go quickly. He held it in his for long, slow beats of time. His gaze went to her mouth as he wondered what it would be like to kiss Carly Bradley. To date Carly. To step into a world of kids and needs… But if it didn't work out, that was a lot of hurting hearts. Too many.

He stepped back.

So did Carly. She held his gaze when she did. "We're neighbors. Friends. But I've got a whole lot of plates spinning right now, and I don't intend to drop any of them. No flirting. None."

He treated it like a gauntlet thrown. "Maybe a little flirting?"

"No." Her voice stayed firm, but he read the temptation in her eyes. "You're facing an uphill battle. So am I. We both need to focus on that."

"Never knew an uphill climb that wasn't better by having two people do it together," he drawled, but he let go of her hand. When he did, his felt empty. He wondered if hers felt the same way.

"Being neighbors and all, we'll be doing that from time to time," she told him, and he caught the note of longing in her voice. Was it bad for two lonely hearts to find one another?

Not bad, his conscience reminded him. *Risky. Tread softly.* Thing was, he didn't want to tread softly. Not anymore.

"Good night, Mike. And again, good job tonight."

He'd set things in motion deliberately because having two deputies involved in game manipulation didn't speak well of those two men or the department. Would they manipulate their jobs the same way? Evidence? Interventions?

He watched Carly cross the road. Lights brightened most of the windows in the small house, and when he turned, the contrast struck him.

His house sat in quiet darkness. Other than the dusk-to-dawn light that oversaw the driveway and carriage barn, his house was unlit.

Usually that hit him hard.

Not tonight. Because standing on the rustic porch, he

realized he had choices now. Choices he hadn't seen for a long time. Opportunities to move forward, into the light.

But he that doeth truth cometh to the light.

The bible verse nudged him.

Carly's door opened from inside as she climbed the steps. Then it clicked softly shut as Jordan left.

And one by one, over the next half hour, the lights went out as kids went to sleep.

He wanted normalcy again. Longed for it. But was he ready to risk his heart?

You might want to think about getting over your anger first, his brain cautioned. *Your brother's a smart man. You might want to take his advice.*

The final light went out in Carly's house and he hadn't even switched one on yet. Could he bridge that gap? Embrace a ready-made family? Face the possible loss of Gracie? Help Carly deal with that possibility?

If you stop thinking about things and start doing them, they get easier.

His father's words. Words to live by.

He wasn't ready to pray for guidance. Not yet, anyway. But the mental reminders struck home because overthinking things made them seem bigger.

He'd been a doer all his life. It was time to step back into that role and then, if things moved forward with his beautiful neighbor, he'd be the kind of man she didn't just need, but the kind of man a wonderful woman like Carly deserved.

Chapter Fourteen

By the time Mike had finished a long shift on Tuesday patrolling Newport, a leftover cold cheeseburger and a two-hour practice with the Under 13 team, he was ready for a good night's sleep.

He dropped the boys off in Carly's driveway.

"Thank you, Coach!" Isaiah always offered a little salute when he thanked Mike for anything, and he always remembered his manners.

Isaac generally needed a reminder, but tonight he turned and high-fived Mike. "Malcolm didn't practice his cheap shots on me tonight, Coach. Thanks for yelling at his dad!"

He started to say he hadn't yelled at anyone, but Isaac was off and running to the house while Isaiah maneuvered his way up the drive with his crutches.

Mike didn't see Carly.

He backed out, assuming she was busy. Bedtime and school were a tough combination when kids got home from practice minutes before they should be in bed.

He grabbed a long, cold glass of tea once he got in the

house, made a couple of overdue phone calls, texted his brother and glanced outside as he headed for the stairs.

A noise drew his attention. A plaintive noise, coming from across the street.

He didn't hesitate. He didn't even think about ignoring the sound. He yanked shoes on and jogged right over.

Carly was on the porch. It was a muggy night, no wind, and the scent of bug spray wafted his way. But it wasn't bug spray that drew him.

Gracie was writhing in Carly's arms, clearly unhappy. She twisted and turned, tears streaming.

When he locked eyes with Carly, the sight of her tiredness blocked everything else. "Hand her over."

"I've got her, I just don't want to keep the others awake, so I brought her outside."

He wasn't about to take no for an answer. "No argument. You're exhausted and there's no sense in you doing this alone when you've got help right here. I'm off tomorrow. I can sleep in if I need to."

"You never sleep in," she scolded.

She was right, but he wasn't about to argue. "All right, but I can still step in here and take care of Gracie while you catch some sleep. Let me take her over to my place. I'll rock her there. That way you guys all get some shut-eye, okay?"

"Mike, I—"

"No arguments, Carly." He reached down and withdrew the sad baby from her arms. "Grab me diapers, some wipes, and get some rest. I've got this. And don't set an alarm, okay?" He felt bad that he hadn't checked on her earlier. He knew Gracie had been suffering from teething and not settling into sleep. Why hadn't he checked up on her?

But he had it in hand now.

He waited for the diaper bag, waved Carly off, and she went. That right there was an indication of how tired she was.

He carried Gracie across the street, took her into the air-conditioned comfort of his big living room and settled into the rocker-recliner he'd bought from the Littletons.

The chair fit like it was made for a dad and a baby girl. It cushioned him and her, and the soft rocking motion was just enough to drift her off to sleep. He didn't know if she dozed off because her pain meds had finally kicked in, or if it was the comfort of the chair, the room and being in his arms, but they snuggled together and woke up nearly seven hours later.

She patted his face around 5:30 a.m. "Bah."

Bottle? Hi? Good morning? 'Sup? Mike had no idea what *bah* meant and he had no milk in the fridge because milk went sour way before he was able to use it. Not like Carly's crew that went through four gallons a week. "Well, good morning to you, too. Feeling better, Gracie?"

A joyous smile crinkled her eyes and showed a flash of the tiny new teeth. "Bah!"

"Glad to hear it. I didn't think about food." He frowned as he righted the recliner. "Oops. Let's go see Mama."

"Bah! Bah! Bah!" she chortled with excitement. Whatever she was saying, the thought of Mama made her even more delighted.

He set her down on the floor while he pulled on his shoes.

Instantly she crawled across the room, grabbed hold of a table leg and pulled herself up. Then she shot him an over-the-shoulder grin, banged on the table and laughed. And this time he didn't think of Wyatt.

All he saw was Gracie, a baby caught in the throes of a custody suit that could turn her life upside down. Would a baby this young be affected by that change? Would she overcome the trauma of being taken from the only mother she'd ever known? And was her biological mother thinking clearly?

He had no answers. Just more questions.

He scooped her up, changed her, and headed across the street just as Carly came out the front door of her place. She was carrying a bottle, and she looked better. Much better.

He grinned. "Great minds think alike."

"I was too tired last night to think at all," she admitted, but she met his grin with a smile. "Thank you so much. I had no idea how much I needed a good night's sleep until I got one. How rough was it?"

"We slept a solid seven hours and never moved— either one of us—so we're in good shape for a busy Wednesday. And this is Hannah's first day at school, correct?"

She grimaced. "Yes, and I'm not sure how that's going to go. Getting on a school bus. Heading off to a place she's only seen once. Change is hard for her."

"Can I come over and help get her on the bus?" he asked. "Or would that make it worse?"

"I have no idea, so why not?" she reasoned. "Coffee?"

He wasn't about to say no. "Yes, ma'am. And plenty of it."

The boys came downstairs a little while later. Isaac looked sleepy. Isaiah appeared ready to greet the day and slay any dragons that might lay in his path.

"You guys are polar opposites in the morning," he noted as he fed Gracie her bottle. Every now and again, she'd pause, reach up and touch his face. Almost as if she were saying thank you for the food. The snuggles. The good night's sleep.

Isaiah looked at the clock then at Mike.

"I kept Gracie at my house last night so your mom could get some sleep," Mike explained. He hadn't thought about the boys being old enough to wonder why he was in their kitchen at dawn's early light. "But I didn't think about a bottle, so here we are."

"She looks happier." Isaac came up alongside. "She's a funny little kid, ain't she?"

Carly cleared her throat.

"Isn't she?" he corrected himself. He rolled his eyes, but when she slipped a freshly toasted bagel with cream cheese in front of him, he sank into a chair. "Thanks, Mom."

Manners. Language skills. Honor. Humor. Love. And food.

His mother had raised them under similar guidelines. Maybe it was a teacher thing, because his mom had taught fifth grade once his little sister started kindergarten. Or it could be a mother thing. In any case, he understood the importance of the combination. With over a quarter century in law enforcement, he'd seen the lack, and that was in no one's best interests. Especially not the kids'.

Gracie finished her bottle, sat herself up and burped.

He smiled at her. "Impressive," he told her.

She laughed, scrambled to get down and crawled to the living room, where she immediately tipped over a box of air-filled plastic balls. They were light enough for her to throw and not break anything, and she plunked herself down, delighted.

The boys caught the bus just as Hannah came out of her room. She saw the bus and the boys. Resigned, she turned toward the kitchen and spotted Mike. "Mike!" She hurried his way. "Mike! Hey, Mike!"

"Well, look at the big girl who goes to school today," Mike told her.

A frown took the place of the smile.

"You get to go to school and play with kids, with toys, to laugh and have fun. Pretty cool, kid."

"Mike. Stay."

Clearly she wasn't on the same page and he wasn't even sure if she understood what he was saying or alluding to. "I'm going to stay with you and Mommy long enough to get you on the bus, okay?"

"Bus gone." She said it dismissively, because the bus had been and gone, and she was still there. Clearly, he was mistaken.

Carly set a piece of cinnamon raisin toast in front of Hannah, and a banana on the side. "Your bus is different," she said. She leaned down and sprinkled Hannah's cheeks with kisses. "It's not as big and it comes later.

We'll walk you out to the bus when it's time, okay? Me, Mike and Gracie."

Hannah ignored her. She looked straight ahead and ate the cinnamon toast then peeled the banana. She said nothing and didn't look left or right, but when it was time to get dressed, she scowled.

"May I help pick out your clothes?" Mike asked her.

She weighed that option, nodded and led the way to her room.

Carly had opened the dresser drawers. A number of cute outfits, tops and bottoms, lined them. "Would you like pink, green or purple today, Hannah-banana?"

Hannah didn't answer Carly, and she didn't acknowledge the rhyming nickname, but she picked up a pair of lilac-toned shorts.

"Purple wins!" Carly kissed her cheek. "Now a top. What top would you like to go with this?"

Lime green won.

"Perfect." Carly didn't push for a matching outfit. She praised the little girl's choice with an approving smile. "Come on out when you're ready and we can get socks and shoes on."

"No socks." Hannah looked horrified by the idea. "No socks."

"Okay, but your feet might feel sore later."

The thought of chafed feet must have loomed better than silly old socks, and when Hannah came into the living room, she crossed over, tugged her shoes into place and stood still, looking nervous.

"Remember how you went to school last year?" asked Carly in a simple conversational tone. "You were in the first year of preschool then. That's what you're going to do this year, only it's a different school and you're in the second year now because you're such a big girl. Isaac and Isaiah are in one school and you'll be in a school just up the road from them, okay?"

Hannah met Carly's gaze.

She didn't look at the road, or outside at all. She took a breath and faced Mike. "Stay?"

"I'll walk you to the bus."

She stood there, not looking around, not meeting his eyes or Carly's. But then she picked up the frog-themed backpack, the one she picked out herself, and moved to the door.

"Let's go." Carly exchanged a look of surprise with Mike. She picked Gracie up and when Mike opened the front door, he half expected Hannah to race for the woods.

She didn't.

She went down the driveway and stood stoically alongside the dog until the rumble of the bus's engine could be heard.

Hannah darted a glance to the left and right, but as the bus came up over the incline, she drew a breath, eyes round, and waited. When the bus door opened, and the driver waved her on, she didn't look back.

She looked forward and moved that way.

Mike didn't know if he should say goodbye or stay quiet. Carly seemed unsure, too, but then she called out in a warm, normal tone, "Have a great day, honey! We love you!"

Hannah turned.

She looked at them, the house and then them again.

She lifted that little chin and her right arm and waved. And then she got on the bus.

When it rolled over the next incline, out of sight, Carly whistled softly. "It can't be that easy."

"Day ain't over," Mike teased. "You might want to avoid the phone."

Gracie reached out then. To him. For him.

A day ago, he'd have avoided the interaction, but not now. He reached out, took her from Carly and settled her on his left hip. "You're talking to Sean today, aren't you?"

"He's calling around ten."

"Need moral support? I've got the day off, remember."

"No."

She turned back toward the house.

"Want me to take Gracie for a little while so you can talk uninterrupted?"

"That would be good." She'd been moving forward, but his offer made her stop. "I have a couple of phone calls to make, the kind that tend to take a while. You don't mind, Mike? You're sure?" She locked eyes with him and he read the sensitivity in her question.

"We bonded last night." He blew raspberry kisses against Gracie's neck and she burst out laughing then hugged him tight. "I'm pretty popular with the girls around here," he bragged, teasing. "Two of them, anyway," he went on. But when he looked into Carly's eyes, he knew it wasn't just two little girls winning his heart.

It was two little girls plus their mama.

She held his gaze.

He held hers. He held it overlong because the last thing he wanted to do was break this connection.

And then he kissed her.

He didn't plan it, but when he read the question in her eyes, the same question plaguing him, he couldn't help it. What would it be like to kiss Carly Bradley? To share time with her? To love her?

Kissing Carly, having her kiss him in return, was the kind of sweetness he'd like to embrace forever. Maybe longer.

He didn't want to break the kiss, but toddler impatience ended the moment when Gracie thumped on his cheek with her little hand.

He sighed.

So did Carly.

And then he laid his forehead to hers. "That was amazing, Carly. Absolutely amazing. And I can't wait until it happens again, darlin'."

Chapter Fifteen

Mike was right. Their kiss was amazing and wonderful, but with so much at stake, a romantic relationship couldn't make the short list. "Agreed. But it can't happen again. You know that."

"Clearly our timing is at odds, because I'm already countin' the minutes till the next time." He smiled down at her. It was so easy to get caught up in his smile, his expression, but worry washed over her.

She kept the explanation simple. "When my marriage fell apart, it nearly broke me, Mike, and my situation is more delicate now. I have four kids to take care of, and one in jeopardy. I have to focus on that. On them. I know you understand."

"So we double the focus," he replied. "More concentrated effort that way. I'm pretty sure as a woman of faith, you might want to figure that maybe God plunked me down here for a reason."

Gracie was bouncing in his arms, ready to be put down to explore the world around her. Carly led the way inside and he set the baby onto the carpet. "I believe in God's timing," she admitted. "I'm not so sure you do, Mike."

His expression turned serious. "I can't dispute that," he said more softly. There was no teasing right now. "Life put me in a chokehold. The worst possible thing happened, made worse because it could have been prevented."

The dog had come inside with them. Barney eyed the baby, did a three-circle spin and curled up by the couch, ready to catch her if she fell.

"I've spent a lot of time being angry," Mike admitted.

"I understand that emotion. But this—" She indicated him and her with a wave. "This has to go on hold. Or be dismissed as wretchedly foolish and utterly dangerous because there are kids involved and they should always come first. Teachers see what happens when kids don't come first. These guys deserve my best, and I can't risk things falling apart. I need you to understand that."

"Then we don't let it fall apart."

"If only it were that easy, but it's not," she replied. "People change. They grow apart, and I never want to be left picking up pieces again. It was hard enough on my own. It's impossible to do with kids counting on me."

"Maybe we're like Isaiah's broken leg."

She frowned because that made no sense.

"When the bone heals, the healed part bonds better because the scarred material is stronger. It makes the leg stronger. You and I aren't kids, Carly."

"The mirror reminds me of that on a regular basis," she noted.

He touched her cheek gently, his look of disbelief

inspiring her smile. Then he acknowledged her with a shrug. "We've both got scars, sure. But we've also got healed bones. And experience. We bring a different set of dynamics to the table. I think that's in our favor."

It was a nice thought, but the anxiety and eating issues that had plagued her when Travis dumped her for another woman had brought up old wounds of childhood rejection. Her emotional reaction to that had toughened her, but it also worried her. "The fact that we're not young means we know enough to take it slow."

"Like midwinter molasses, if that's what it takes, ma'am." He grinned, which eased the knot of worry somewhat. "Some things are worth waiting for. I expect this is one of those times. And a gentleman isn't afraid to do some old-fashioned courting with the woman in question."

She'd gone into the boys' adoption fully expecting to be a single mother for the rest of her days. Then Mike rolled into town and into their hearts. "We're a lot to take on," she warned him.

He winked. "My mama raised me to be up for any challenge."

"And I'm never one to argue with mamas." She smiled at him.

He smiled back and moved to the door. "I'll come back for Gracie so you can make your calls, okay? Here's hoping Hannah will have a good day at school. You know how you were looking for more information on her?"

"Yes."

"Would the former school ship records to the pre-K she's going to now?" he wondered aloud.

"It might," she replied. "That's one of the calls I'm making. I'll put in the request, but being a foster mother carries little weight. I can't make them do it. It has to come from their county worker. We'll see."

"If at first you don't succeed…" He headed for the door.

"Exactly."

Gracie dozed off on the carpet a few minutes later, her head resting along Barney's flank. She stayed asleep as Carly picked her up, brought her to her room and tucked her into bed. Her nap gave Carly time to clean up, load the dishwasher, apply a little much-needed makeup and blow-dry her hair.

She didn't think about the last time she'd worried about makeup or hair. That was no one's business. The fact that it meant something now was reason enough to do it.

Mike picked up Gracie as promised. He shifted her car seat into his SUV and took off for town, so when Sean called ten minutes later, the house was quiet.

Carly knew the moment she heard his voice that the news wasn't good. "The judge is due back in twelve days," he told her in a quiet voice. "But his clerk has gone over the petition and the notes and said there's little wiggle room on this. Gracie's mother is within her rights and the legal time frame. She's maintained her nonaddicted status since Gracie's birth, and that's six months post-incarceration. That's the kind of good faith a judge looks for. It doesn't look promising, Carly. I'm sorry."

"Can I talk to her? Appeal to her? Cut a deal of some kind, Sean?" she asked. "Does she understand the repercussions for the other three? How will they feel when they lose their baby sister? And why weren't the older kids important enough to also seek custody? You've got kids, Sean. You know they'll come up with a lot more questions and self-doubts over time. And what happens if she starts using again? Who looks out for Gracie's best interests then?"

She was caught in the middle of an impossible situation. She understood the yearning to be a mother. It was natural for Lida to want her baby back, but Gracie was only part of the family equation. The other three kids were just as important.

She thanked Sean for his help and asked him to check in with Hannah's former social worker. "I'm hoping the weight of your title makes a difference," she explained. "I've gotten nowhere. I have no way to talk to the former foster mother or professionals who might have worked with Hannah, and I'm walking in the dark with this child. I'm just looking for insight. It would be a huge help to have some background information on Hannah to help me address her emotional issues. When the adoption is finalized, I have more rights, but I'm in limbo right now if I can't get authorities to speak on my behalf."

"Summer's always tough," he assured her. "People take vacations and everyone in Human Services is short-staffed. Now that school's back in session, we should see a difference, but I'll see what I can do to free things up. And, Carly, I just want to say that I'm impressed. Few people open their hearts and homes to four kids, especially older boys like Isaiah and Isaac. It's pretty cool."

It was a lovely compliment but Sean had it backward. "I'm the fortunate one. The day the boys' adoption was finalized was the happiest day of my life. That blessing goes both ways."

"I'll get back to you when I know more."

She hung up, called Hannah's former school and again got nowhere. She'd expected that, but filed a request for their counselor to talk to the Kendrick Creek pre-K counselor. If the professionals made contact, they might get things moving in the right direction for Hannah's needs. If they didn't, Carly would push until they did.

Why not do that with Gracie?

The question pressed her to think wider. Broader.

She'd been given preferential options for Gracie and Hannah because she'd adopted their brothers. Why not press to make that same law work in reverse?

She called Janice and waded right in when the social worker answered. "It's Carly, Janice. I heard from my lawyer that the judge has a very narrow scope of choices with Lida's petition for Gracie. It leans in her favor."

Janice hesitated then agreed. "It's true enough. The Family Preservation Act doesn't give a real choice, Carly."

"Except where do siblings' rights fall in the equation? They're family, too."

"They aren't considered a direct part of the process."

"So they're sidelined."

"In a way. Yes."

Carly wasn't about to give up. "And yet Gracie is with me because of a caveat inspired by the same law. I was sought out because I had her brothers, so I was given first option to adopt her. The boys had legal standing then. Why not now? Children aren't second-class citizens."

"Oh, sugar, babies don't vote," Janice said dryly. "And that's a fact we can't overlook. Most don't choose to fight the system because there's no glory in fighting a losing battle. I'm sorry but I've got to go, I have an intake just outside of Newport in ten minutes, but I will keep you updated. I promise. And I'll keep praying." She ended the call.

Janice believed in the power of prayer, the strength of family, and she was a single mother. Her husband had died after wounds suffered in a military training accident six years before. She was raising two girls on her own, and she understood the constraints of time, money and work.

Carly plugged the phone in to charge it and walked outside.

Midsummer noises surrounded her. The birds didn't sing in the heat of the day. This was locust weather, and their drone had marked the start of school for as long as she could remember. Isaiah. Isaac. And now Hannah. All in school, all day, five days a week and now—

Tears didn't just threaten. They flowed. She crossed the porch to the small glider and sank down as the reality broadsided her.

She would lose Gracie.

Her chest tightened at the thought of handing the baby over to Lida. Her righteous nature warred with her motherly instincts. Was she wrong to fight this? Or was it more wrong to step aside, knowing how difficult Lida's life had been? And should adults get unlimited chances when it came to children's health and happiness?

She didn't know the answers, but she knew who would. She picked up her phone and called Sean Morris back.

He answered right away. "Carly. Hey. What's up? Did you get some results on Hannah already?"

"No. I'm not calling about Hannah, Sean. I'm calling about Gracie."

"Yes?" She heard the hesitancy in his tone but then he said, "I'm listening."

She explained her phone call with Janice and the law. "So here's the thing," she challenged. "I'm not a lawyer. This is your skill set. So tell me, Sean, why isn't removing one child from a sibling group weighed into the overall decision of where a child should go? Why don't those siblings matter under the law? Because if it's truly a law aimed at family preservation, all parts of the family should have equal weight."

"It doesn't work that way."

"Exactly!" she exclaimed. "Which is why I need to make this not just a case, but a cause. A true cause of standing up for children's rights, for their right to be part of the family. Doesn't my adoption of the boys set a precedent?"

"Yes. In a way."

"So there we are," she told him frankly. "I want to counterpetition. And I don't want it based on having Gracie for nearly nine months, because Lida's claim will negate that. But if we refile because seventy-five percent of Gracie's family is with me, we can set the precedent for putting children's rights front and center, where they should be."

Sean's voice took an upward tick. "That precedent could offer grounds for appeal if we lose initially."

"Because how does one law serve two masters?" she asked. "It can't. And, Sean, I'm not rich. I'm doing all right, but a teacher doesn't make a fortune. You know that. But I've studied enough history to hope this could be groundbreaking."

"We're talking a case that could end up changing the law of the land," he said frankly. "And that means a lot of invested hours. I don't think either of us can afford that."

"I can't afford *not* to do it," she told him. "Because it's the right thing to do. If I need to start an online fundraiser, I'll do it because children should have rights. The way things stand currently, their rights are shoved aside. We can change that. If you're willing."

He said nothing for a moment, then clicked his tongue, a trend she'd noticed in his office a few weeks before. "Let me think on it, okay? Not because I don't think we should do it, but I need to check with my partners. And we don't want bad stuff kicked back on the other three kids. There could be truths that come out about their mother that would be emotionally harmful to them."

Years of teaching had shown Carly the truth in that. "It's hard to know when to push forward and when to let go, but the boys lived it. They haven't forgotten what it was like. Think about it, please. And get back to me."

"I'll call you by tomorrow."

"Thank you."

"And pray, Carly. For all of us."

That part wasn't a problem. "I sure will."

Mike brought Gracie back to the house at lunchtime. He'd grabbed a pizza at the local convenience store that, surprisingly, made really good pizza. Carly was on the porch when he pulled in. Eyes down, she was busily typing on her laptop.

She was beautiful, sitting there, cross-legged, wearing shorts and a tank top. Reading glasses in place, she was focused on the task at hand, but she pushed them up as he came closer with Gracie.

He frowned. "You've been crying. What's wrong? What's happened? How can I help?"

She waved her hand. "I was crying because I was angry. Now I'm motivated and, if your brother is willing to help me, I'm going to take on the law of the land, Mike. If he can't help, I'll find someone who will, because it's an awful thing to ignore the needs of three-quarters of a family to fulfill the wishes of one member. And that needs to change."

"I don't understand," he admitted, then jiggled Gracie a little. "And my little friend needs lunch. She likes to eat."

"Oh, she sure does, my little Gracie-baby." Carly stood and tucked the laptop beneath her arm. "I've got her food ready inside. If you settle her into the high chair, I can explain my plan while I feed her."

"Sounds good." Mike strapped her into the chair when they got to the kitchen. He retrieved the pizza and set it on the counter separating the kitchen from the dining area. "I changed her at the station."

"You took her to the courthouse?" she asked, surprised.

"Thought it might be good for the guys to see I'm human."

"Using the baby as a prop." She sat to feed Gracie and lifted one eyebrow in Mike's direction. "Well played."

"But with sincere intent," Mike replied. "Definitely not indiscriminate use."

Carly laughed. "Hey, if it scored you some points with the guys, that's wonderful, and I'm sure it was an adventure for Gracie."

"People made a massive fuss over her, and she didn't fall apart."

"No?" Carly leaned forward and kissed the baby's soft cheek. "Well done, pudding!"

He brought the conversation back to whatever had upset her. After serving in the juvenile crime unit for years, Mike knew that kids and the legal system were a volatile mix for families. "So what made you cry, Carly? And should I kill them outright or torture them first? I'm okay either way."

She scoffed. "Not true, you're a gentle giant, but thank you for jumping to my defense. I want to file a countersuit for custody of Gracie, citing the boys' and Hannah's rights to maintain their family. I can't believe that the law that brought the children to me is the same one that allows one of them to be taken back, so I've asked Sean to push that angle."

"And he agreed?" asked Mike, because Sean wasn't a jump-in-with-both-feet kind of guy. He looked before he leapt.

"Not yet, but if he doesn't, I'll find someone who does because the rights of children shouldn't be over-shadowed. They have the right to be a family. I'm determined," she finished.

Then she looked up at him. He read the resolve in her gaze, but her next words stopped him cold. "I've been praying for how best to fight this. Not because I don't like Lida. I don't know her. And she's blessed me with four kids. But I know how badly I fell apart after my husband cheated on me and left. I crashed, Mike. Totally. I starved myself, trying to become thinner and prettier. It wasn't until the therapist made me see that it was Travis's choices and not my lack that I could start being okay again. Eating more healthily. Being constantly shuffled around and rejected as a child created triggers. Travis's cheating set them all on fire and I couldn't handle it. I fell apart before I reached out for help. It wasn't a short walk back, but I did it," she told him as Gracie gobbled her food.

Normally, Mike would have laughed at the baby's greedy antics.

Not now.

Not when Carly was laying down the very sword he could never pick up again.

"I was afraid to make waves because I didn't want to instigate a relapse, but I realized today that I'm strong enough. I have to be, because there is no one else that can go to bat for these kids. And I'm willing to do it." She reached out a soft damp cloth to wipe food from Gracie's face and looked up at Mike. She read his look and her expression shifted. "Are you okay?"

He wasn't okay.

He didn't know what he was, but okay had nothing to do with it.

His chest had gone tight. He wasn't even sure he could breathe because the weight on his heart was like a thousand stacked boulders pressing in. "Fine."

He wasn't fine. He was the opposite of fine.

He got up from the table and headed for the door. "Gotta go. I'll pick up the boys for practice later."

He didn't look back to see her reaction. He couldn't. Because if he did, she'd see his.

He climbed into his SUV and drove. He didn't drive anywhere in particular; he just drove. He did it for hours, wondering how this had happened.

What were the odds that the woman he'd fallen in love with, the woman of strength with a heart of gold, fought the same eating disorder that his wife had had?

Impossible odds. And yet, not impossible because they happened. They were real. And the look on her face when he'd told her he was fine—

Despite his big words about defending her no matter what, he was running scared. And the truth of that might be the scariest thing of all.

Chapter Sixteen

He pulled into her driveway at 5:40 p.m. as usual.

The boys hustled out to the SUV.

Carly didn't.

Just as well, he reasoned as he drove toward town. There was nothing he could say or do to fix this. Not when it was as bad as it could possibly get.

He dropped the boys off at her house after practice, went home and shut the door. Practice times were halved once school started, so there would be a decent window of time before the kids were inside for the night.

He didn't want to hear voices coming from across the street. He didn't want to hear her call the boys in or let the dog out.

He sat and put his head in his hands, with no idea what to do. How could he stay in this house now? How could he be the law enforcement leader he needed to be for this community if he was constantly worried about Carly? How could he function?

As he contemplated scenarios, his phone rang. It

was one of the assistant chiefs of police from Nashville Metro. He leaned back in the chair and took the call.

"Mike, that Midtown job you and I talked about is opening up in six weeks. It's on the down-low, buddy, but we want you back here. It's yours for the asking. Dunlevy is retiring and our vote for you was unanimous, so I said I'd call. We need you, Mike. Your city needs you. Come on home."

It was an answer to prayer—only he hadn't prayed and wasn't about to. Praying was something others did, the ones who couldn't rely on themselves to get things done. He'd been born getting things done. Born to lead, to guard, to protect. He'd known that from the time he was a kid on safety patrol outside the elementary school he'd attended for eight years.

He *could* go back. His former commander was offering him a way out at the best possible time. That couldn't be a coincidence.

He'd lose some rent on the Littleton house. No huge deal there, fortunately.

Then his gaze fell on the playbook sitting on the kitchen island.

His heart sank.

The house rent wasn't a big deal. The football team was.

And as much as he knew things couldn't be as he'd hoped just hours before, Carly and those kids mattered. All the kids mattered, but particularly the Bradley bunch across the street.

"You don't have to decide now," Vickers told him. "Take a few days. I know you've been wrestlin' the devil, Mike, and I'm not minimizing that, but we need you here. You're part of Nashville's finest and you always will be. You're appreciated here, Mike, but I'm not trying to talk you into it. You think about it a few days and let me know."

"I'll do that. And thanks, Chief."

"Talk to you soon."

He put down the phone.

The outside dusk-to-dawn lights came on, illuminating the hillside lot around him. Carly's did the same a few moments later.

His dream job. The city he loved. Memories he'd loved and those he had a hard time facing.

He stared at the phone. Why now? Why had this call come when he most needed it?

Or maybe it came when it was most tempting? argued the other side of his brain. *Maybe it came when you're most vulnerable.*

He hated feeling vulnerable. He'd spent decades being a guardian until it all washed out beneath him because he wasn't able to save or protect those who'd needed him most.

Mike went to work the next day after little sleep. There was no practice that night, and when he received a short text from Carly that she'd drop the boys at practice on Friday night, he sent her a simple checkmark response.

She didn't come to the game on Sunday. Isaiah was on the sidelines as usual, with his crutches. Isaac had played in his game earlier in the day, but when Mike scanned the bleachers for Carly, Hannah and Gracie, they weren't there.

His fault, he knew.

They won the game by a narrow margin. It should have felt good. The kids were ecstatic and the town was happy, but a gridiron win didn't fill the emptiness inside him.

He had two days off after a Sunday evening shift. It was time to seek advice from the one person who was never afraid to set him square as needed.

His mother.

He drove straight to his parents' ranch north of Nashville on Monday morning. Morris Acres sat atop a knoll. It gave his mother a view she loved and the privacy she craved after being raised by various family members in Memphis.

It had been his home for over twenty years, a great place to raise a family.

He parked the SUV between the barn and the house. He walked inside. The smell of coffee hit him square, while a tray of fresh-baked cookies sat cooling on the kitchen counter. He grabbed two, then realized he didn't remember eating the previous day. Coffee, yes. Food, no. And he hadn't thought about it much, either.

"Sit." His mother pointed to the scarred and beloved kitchen table and set a mug of coffee in front of him. "Don't fill up on cookies. I've got fresh turkey for sandwiches. Or ham. What's going on?"

"Vickers offered me the Midtown Hills' command."

His mother whistled softly. "Why are they tempting you now?"

He made a face. "I'm not sure. I figured you'd see it as God's timing."

She rolled her eyes. "That would be convenient, wouldn't it? And it's a great honor to have it offered.

But you didn't go to Kendrick Creek on a whim, and the reasons you left here haven't changed. But maybe *you* have?"

She posed the question like she always did. Quietly. Calmly. Leading a big, busy family for more than half a century.

"Still the same guy."

She sipped her coffee and stayed quiet.

"The sheriff's department is different," he explained without explaining anything. "Real different."

"In a bad way?"

He shook his head instantly. "No. The guys aren't exactly fawning over me, but then, I grabbed a job, took over coaching their beloved football team and thwarted some of their less stellar coaching practices."

"Reason enough to hate you right there," Jerusha replied. "I know a little bit about men and sports and winning records. I raised a few boys of my own."

He grimaced. "Correct. It is different, and maybe I'm not meant to do different. Maybe I'm meant to stay here, command a precinct and go on with my life. That's not a bad option, is it?"

"It's a great option," she reasoned. Then she added a caveat. "If that's what you want."

It wasn't what he wanted, but he couldn't have what he wanted, so why belabor it? "Maybe *want* doesn't enter into the equation. Maybe *need* outweighs want."

Her ludicrous expression underscored her opinion on that statement. "That's about the dumbest thing you've said in a while."

He drew back. "That's coming from the woman who is always helping others? Always saying yes?"

"At my age I have the option of saying yes to a lot of things," she said sensibly. "If that's what you were doing, I'd say go for it. And your daddy would agree," she assured him. "But that's not exactly the situation here. Is it?"

They exchanged looks. He growled. "Sean's got a big mouth."

"He loves his brother and doesn't understand why you fell off the grid two days ago when he tried to set up a meeting with you and a woman named Carly? About a baby adoption and taking on the courts?"

"Sean had no right to lay this at your door."

"Or he did the right thing and intervened before you manage to ruin something downright beautiful. Would you like to talk? Or saddle up and ride, then talk?"

"I don't want to talk at all."

"Except you came here to talk," she mused as she slapped ham and turkey onto a sandwich. "So it must be the subject matter that's got you in a tizzy."

He wasn't in a tizzy. He was hurt. Angry. Ticked off…

Okay, he *was* in a tizzy, but a ride and a sandwich and a chat with good old Mom wasn't going to fix anything because he couldn't fix the unfixable.

No one could.

No one could turn back time and—

The pastor's words flooded over him. *It's a rugged world. Good stuff and bad stuff happens every day. Faith can strengthen us to hold strong in the hard times, but hard times are part of the equation.*

Was he the one holding the empty oil lamp he used to

hear about as a kid? Was he the one expecting answers to unanswerable questions and giving up?

"Mike, you've gone your own way for a long while." His mother set the sandwich down in front of him. "I pray about it. I ask God to watch over you every single day, not because of your job, although I know the dangers there. I pray because you're so determined to chart your own path, which makes sense to you because you're so dependable. You've been able to do it so far, but life hands out some tough roads and I don't know where I'd be now if it weren't for that rock of faith I yammer on about.

"Now it's up to you," she said as she settled into the chair alongside him. She was wearing her typical T-shirt and capris, clothes that didn't get in her way for working on the farm. "I don't know what's going on in Kendrick Creek, but moving there was the first positive step you've made since we lost Hallie and the baby. I watched you flounder, Michael."

His hands shook as she spoke because he didn't flounder as a rule. Lately he felt like that was all he'd been doing.

Until you raced across the street a few weeks ago.

His heart beat faster. He'd felt good for a while there. Real good, in so many ways. Hopeful.

"But I know that Sean said you seemed like yourself for the first time in a long time, maybe even a better version of yourself because you were helping a woman with a bunch of kids."

"She's got an eating disorder." He blurted the words because the truth of them stabbed him. "She told me last week, just out of the blue, how she and Sean were planning on taking on the legal establishment to keep Gracie—she's the baby," he explained. "She's almost nine months old now, and she's been with Carly and the boys from the time she was born, and then Carly explains how she almost killed herself by starving herself when her marriage fell apart and instead of helping her, I ran."

"You intend to stay gone, Michael?" asked his mother. She wasn't one to mince words. "Or do you mean to stand tall and strong and fight for this baby with every ounce you've got? Because if ever a woman could use a strong man at her side, it's when she's fighting the system. You know I didn't have a family life growing up. I've said that often enough."

"Yes." His mother had been bounced from home to home, some with family, some with government placements.

"I'd have given anything to have a place to call home. To have a family that loved me, that saw the good in me. When I married your father, that became my singular goal. To have the kind of home I never had, with all the squabbles and hugs and slammed doors that go along with it. I haven't bossed you around in a good long time," she noted firmly, "but if I were of a mind to do it now, I'd say eat your sandwich, slug some coffee and head back east to make things right. Opportunities for love aren't a dime a dozen and if you squander them, that's on you. And that's all I'm going to say."

She was right, as usual.

She packaged up a plastic container of cookies and by the time he'd eaten she had a to-go cup filled with coffee. "I'd like to come your way and meet this gal,

Michael. If she doesn't toss you out the door and turn the key."

"No more than I deserve, but if I stop acting like a jerk and turn on the Morris charm…"

"Charm comes from my side, not the Morrises, but either way…" She reached up and hugged him when he stood. "Grab on to faith, grab on to family and shrug off stubbornness. Now, that's a Morris trait," she added firmly. "The good Lord knows I've dealt with that with your daddy often enough."

"Tell Dad I love him."

"Will do. And drive safe."

He didn't stay to ride or see his father or visit old haunts.

He got into that SUV and drove straight back to Kendrick Creek where he belonged.

What could he say to Carly?

The truth.

Once told, would she have him? Forgive him?

Maybe. That was up to her. But his goal was to make himself as forgivable as possible because his mother was right. Standing up and fighting for Carly and those kids was what he should have done all along. It would be up to her whether he got the second chance he wanted.

Chapter Seventeen

Carly ran to the grocery store Sunday evening. Isaiah was watching the kids and she had a long list that couldn't wait until Monday. She'd just grabbed fruit and bread when she ran into Crystal Kennedy.

"Late shopping, too?" Crystal sent her a look of empathy. "What on earth are we gonna do if our new coach takes that big job back in Nashville?"

Big job in Nashville?

Carly hoped she didn't look as blank as she felt. She settled a bag of cucumbers she didn't want into her cart and said, "It's a conundrum, isn't it?"

"That is exactly what it is," declared Crystal. "We are caught betwixt and between, and my Jed says that Mike Morris is what the county needs these days, a fellow who won't twist this and that to suit the current moment. There's a reason for rules," she continued. "Mame Haney over at the clerk's office said Mike was on the books as a temporary hire, so maybe the city got him back by dangling that big job and bigger paycheck. I love goin' to Nashville," she added, as if confiding in a good friend. They weren't really friends, but Crystal was a good sort that loved to talk and her husband, Jed, was salt of the earth.

"But living there wouldn't make the short list, if you know what I mean. I love our town, but being raised there, it's different for him. Anyway, I hope he doesn't take the offer. He coached a good game today, I'll say that. Real good. Although we're all waitin' on your boy gettin' back to playin'," she declared firmly. "That's for certain. You do well with those children, Carly, and I'm always amazed because you make it look easy and bein' a mom is anything but." She grabbed a bag of green grapes and headed up front. "See you later this week."

Here temporarily.

A big job in Nashville.

He'd said never a word to her that he might be leaving.

Carly wasn't sure she grabbed what she needed, but two pints of her favorite ice cream went into that cart and, as soon as she did that, guilt set in. Guilt about the ice cream, about wanting it, about not daring to have it. For a moment, she stared at her cart, confounded, but then she pushed it up front, paid for her groceries and went home.

He'd stunned her when he walked out of the house the other day.

He'd gotten that blank look of disbelief, done a quick pivot and walked out the door. And hadn't come back.

You fell for him. You know better, and still you fell for him. Hook, line and sinker. What were you thinking?

Dumb. She knew that now and should have known

then because wonderful, caring, compassionate men didn't just appear out of nowhere.

Where exactly do they come from?

She refused her brain the dignity of an answer because maybe they didn't come from anywhere. Maybe they didn't exist. Wasn't that the very reason she avoided all those stupid happy-ending movies? They were works of fiction and Carly's current reality was to save her family. One way or another, she was going to do it.

She didn't need Mike Morris.

She didn't need his affection, his strength, his humor, his devotion.

She didn't—

She fought tears as she put the groceries away.

She fought tears the next morning while Gracie napped.

She fought them when Hannah stared out the front window, waiting to see her hero come strolling up the driveway. When the driveway stayed stubbornly empty and tiny tears slipped down Hannah's pale cheeks, Carly stopped fighting tears.

She fought anger.

How dare he ingratiate himself to a little child then walk away? Was the idea of fighting the system anathema to a man of law?

Well, too bad.

She'd avoided him purposely since he'd walked out. She took the boys to Friday night practice and took the girls home after Isaac's Sunday game. She had no intention of staying and watching while Mike ignored her, ignored the kids and kept his distance.

She'd held it together throughout the weekend, but

by the time the kids got onto the school bus Monday morning, she let herself cave for a little while, but not too long because there were things to do.

She cleaned the kitchen and wrote several emails to local news organizations highlighting the problems relating to children through current custody laws. Once Gracie was awake, Carly fed her and despite the baby's endearing antics, she still felt like punching someone.

There was a time when she would have just called Jordan and dished, but there was too much at stake now. She loved her friend but the memory of how she'd crashed when Travis cheated had taught Carly a valuable lesson. She'd learned to have a plan in place, so she didn't call Jordan. She called her therapist and set up an appointment for the following day.

Mike's leaving was on him. Not her.

Part of her brain believed that, but another part of her head wasn't buying it. Not for one cotton-picking minute. Because she'd fallen for him.

And she thought he felt the same.

Stop rehashing this, her brain scolded. *It is what it is and there are so many things to do. You have a fundraiser to plan and laws to change. Get on it.*

She'd completed most of her tasks by midday.

Sean was initiating the new petition; she'd voiced her opinion publicly through social media and the two local papers. The town businesses had sidewalk displays planned. The food trucks and Hidey's Barbecue were scheduled for the church grounds, and she was printing out two-hundred-and-fifty trifold pamphlets as fundraiser handouts. But when her low-ink light turned on, she went straight back to wanting to punch someone. Or something.

Mike had offered to donate two new cartridges to the cause, but now Mike was gone, the ink was going to run out and there were no local stores that carried ink cartridges for her printer—or any printer, for that matter. That meant a trip to Newport or Sevierville, a trip she didn't have time to make before practice that evening.

Irritation spiraled up Carly's spine.

She choked a solid lump in her throat down, blinked back tears because she'd shed enough of them, and stirred the pasta she'd started for a quick-fix casserole when Hannah let out a cry of joy. "Mike!" she yelled through the big front window in a gleeful voice. "Mike! Mike! Mike!"

The little girl raced for the door. The lock stymied her. She stomped her feet, desperate to get to her buddy.

Carly didn't want to unlatch the door. It would be too much like unlatching her heart, and her emotions were nothing to be toyed with. Ever.

But Hannah needed closure, so Carly unhooked the upper lock and opened the door.

Hannah raced across the narrow porch and down the steps.

Mike scooped her up and the four-year-old wrapped her arms around his neck as if to never let go, but Carly knew it wasn't Hannah's choice.

It was Mike's and he'd already walked away once. Once was all you got.

He met her gaze over Hannah's soft brown hair. "Can we talk?"

Not in this lifetime.

That's what she wanted to say, but she bit her tongue. "Nothing to be said, neighbor. Actions speak louder than words."

"And sometimes words spur actions," he replied.

Carly wasn't in the mood for riddles or a blame game. "Fortunately, therapy has taught me to separate my guilt from others' actions," she said smoothly. "It was a good lesson. One I'm not afraid to put into action," she stated. "Thanks for being a good neighbor, Mike." Cool, calm and collected. That's how she'd wanted to sound, and she'd pulled it off. "It's been appreciated. And now, Hannah-banana, we've got to get things done inside. Come with Mama."

Hannah responded by tightening her grip like a spider monkey clinging to its mother's back. "Mike," she insisted. She darted a dark look at Carly. "My Mike," she declared, entwining those fingers as tightly as she could at the back of his neck. "My very own Mike."

A four-word sentence.

Carly stared at Hannah. "Hannah, that was good talking. Beautiful words, sweetheart. So well done."

Hannah wasn't buying into the compliment because Carly still had her arms out to remove the little girl from Mike's arms. "Mike stay. Hannah stay." She stared at Carly, daring her to misinterpret the words. "My Mike."

Carly wished it were that easy. It wasn't. She reached up to unwind Hannah's arms. "And Mike's our neighbor, so we'll see him because he'll be right across the street. For now."

She locked eyes with Mike deliberately and when he stayed calm, he almost got a kick in the shins. She might have done exactly that if Hannah weren't there. "Come on, puddin'. Let's go make supper. The pasta!" She'd forgotten it, left it boiling, and by now it would be mush.

She raced inside and when she drained the mushy noodles, she wanted to throw the stupid strainer across the room. And maybe the pot, too. Just because.

She didn't because cool, collected moms handled things.

She set a fresh pot of water on, took a breath and turned toward the living room.

Mike had followed her in. He wisely didn't offer to help.

He unwound Hannah from his neck, set her down, then crouched low. "Listen, I've got to go do some things now, okay?"

Hannah's face darkened.

"But I'll be around tomorrow and the next day and the day after that, all right?"

Hannah's chin quivered. Her eyes went round. "Mike stay."

The wistful look on Hannah's face broadsided Carly. She saw herself in that expression; a little child, longing for love and stability. The little one held Mike's gaze, wanting to communicate with him but stymied. "Please."

"I'll be back, okay? Promise."

"She needs honesty, Mike."

Mike looked up. Locked eyes with Carly. "I know."

Sure he did, but he was making a promise to a compromised child who wouldn't understand the empty house across the street when Mike headed west to Nashville. "If you're headed back to Nashville, she needs to understand that. She needs transition time. It's better to be open with her."

He stood and met her gaze. "Exactly what I'm doing. She's here and I'm here. For the long haul. And, yes, I was offered a job in Nashville. I turned it down. I'm here to stay."

Carly wasn't sure if that made things better or worse. If he were gone, the steady reminders went with him. If he stayed, his positions and proximity meant she couldn't get away from him.

"We still need that talk," he told her. He kissed Hannah's head and ruffled her hair before he moved to the door. "Miss Hannah, I will see you tomorrow, okay? You be good for Mama."

"'Amorrow." She gave him a hard stare that meant business. "See you 'amorrow."

Mike grinned, bent low and hugged her. "Good talking! Well done. Yes, I'll see you tomorrow. Oh, wait. I almost forgot."

He reached into his pocket, withdrew two new ink cartridges and set them on the side table near the door. "I took them out of the packaging because it's a pain to open. Black and tricolor. Right?"

He'd remembered his promise.

She stayed where she was and nodded. "Yes."

"I'll be back, ladies."

Hannah clasped her hands, this time in joy, while emotions steamrolled Carly.

Hannah's talking was a monumental step forward, but was it spurred by Mike's return? Or natural attribution of words as she grew more comfortable with Carly?

Either way, it was a marvelous thing and they needed

to encourage it. But why did Mike Morris have to be the one to inspire it?

Shouldn't you just be glad she's trying and succeeding?

The common sense of the mental scolding made her frown, but when Gracie crawled over to ruin the tiny animal setup Hannah had created, Hannah stood, put her hands on her hips and said, "No, baby. No. Mustn't touch."

Isaiah had just hobbled downstairs.

Isaac was shooting hoops outside.

Isaiah crossed to the door and yelled his brother's name. "Isaac! Come here! Hannah's talking!"

"For real?" Isaac tossed the ball into the grass, left Barney on watch detail and raced inside. "You talking, kiddo? Well, it's about time!" He laughed and hugged her.

Hannah didn't like hugs, but she let him.

Then Isaiah scooped her up and said, "Hey, little sister, good job! You've got words, girl!"

She smiled up at him.

He raised her high and she almost laughed. And then he set her down near the miniature creatures she'd arranged in her corner. "You know I used to play with little dudes like that when I was your age. Bunnies, bears and dogs. 'Til they got sold for drug money."

He didn't have to say the rest. His mother's addictions had ruled their early years.

He turned, crossed the room and hugged Carly. "If I forget to say it sometimes, thank you." He hugged her tight and she had to fight back tears. Again. "For taking us. For all this. Just thanks, Mom."

She hugged him back then batted him in the arm. "Don't get me all sentimental, brat. I've got things to do."

"And I saw Coach's car pull in across the street. I want to talk to him before practice."

"Me, too." Isaac called Barney in, then the boys crossed the street.

She didn't stop them. That would be dumb. If Mike was staying, the boys would continue a relationship with him. He was their coach. A mentor. And a good male role model, something they'd never had.

But if she happened to draw mustaches and bunny ears on his picture in the wee small hours, that was her choice. Juvenile but quite effective.

She got home from her therapy session at lunchtime the next day.

Jordan had taken Gracie to play with the Trembeth girls while Carly kept her appointment and finished up pre-fundraiser prep work.

A familiar whistle came her way as she climbed out of the car.

She turned, annoyed. She thought he'd be working. She thought she'd have the afternoon to absorb the therapist's uplifting words and sage advice. But when she spotted Mike coming her way, torn emotions grabbed hold.

Kick him or kiss him?

Neither was right, and raw reactions were often unacceptable. It's what a person did in lieu of the raw reaction that made them socially normal, so she did neither. She waited as he drew close and put in place her most professional closed face, the one she saved for the most obnoxious people on the planet.

"Is this a good time?" he asked.

She pretended to be obtuse. "For?"

His left brow arched slightly. "For us to talk?"

"Nothing to say, Mike. I've got nothing to say and nothing I care to hear." She started for the house.

So did he. "You know I'm a widower."

Only a total jerk could walk away from that opening, so she stopped and turned back. "Yes. And I'm sorry, Mike. Sincerely sorry."

"I know." He looked at her, then beyond her, before drawing his gaze back to hers. "Hallie was ten years younger than me. We met when I was called in to break up a fight at a club across the street from her apartment. She was funny. Bright. Sassy. And filled with faith," he went on. He frowned. "It's weird that I didn't see what a big part of her that was, her faith, her joy in being part of life, part of a church, part of everything. If you knew the grown-up version of her, you'd never know that she spent the better part of two years fighting for her life when she was a teen." He paused slightly before he went further.

"She was anorexic. She never showed me pictures of what she went through, or how twisted the mind gets when the image we see isn't the image that's real. She was so beautifully normal, healthy and happy that I viewed the past for what it was—something that happened a long time before. We got married and it was wonderful. Really wonderful. But then we got stymied trying to have a family."

"It's like that for a lot of people these days."

"I didn't know anything about it until it happened to us," he admitted. "We went to a clinic, we jumped through a gazillion hoops and they managed what had seemed impossible for years: we were expecting. I can't tell you how happy that made me," he explained in that strong, gentle voice. "Both of us. It was better than Olympic gold or a Super Bowl win or a World Series ring. Not one of those options meant more than having that baby with my wife. And then..."

He got quiet. Looked away. Then sighed. "She was gone. Our son was gone. Just like that. With no warning, no symptoms, no anything. Her heart failed and I lost them both instantly. And then I found out that the regular obstetrician had no idea she'd had a severe eating disorder when she was a teen. Somehow that fact was never brought to their attention. They didn't look at her heart the way they would have if they'd known. They could have monitored her. Put her in the hospital or birthing center and kept her under watch just in case. But they hadn't known. And I've never been so angry in my life."

Carly didn't try to comfort him. Didn't try to make it better, because there was nothing that could make it better.

"A simple note on a current chart could have kept my world intact. And it never happened.

"I was furious," he told her. "With God, for being stupid. With the doctors and their staff, for being negligent and not doing their duty. And with me, for not making sure everything that could be done was done. We'd failed her. We'd failed that baby. We'd failed at life. And that meant I'd failed."

He drew a deep breath and held her gaze. "I couldn't move on. Couldn't breathe like a normal person. Couldn't get up out of bed every day as if I had something to live for, because I didn't. I functioned by doing exactly what had to be done because that was all I could manage. And then Sean and Pastor Bob made me think."

His jaw flexed slightly. "They made me see that maybe it was Hallie I was mad at and couldn't admit it, because why didn't she make sure the chart was up to date? Why didn't she tell them? And the minute they said that, I knew why, Carly." He frowned.

"She wanted to be like all the other expectant mothers, enjoying each moment, each twinge, each kick, each thrill. Of course, she had no idea that it could end badly. I know that because she hated that part of her life, so when you mentioned your problem last week, I crashed."

The heartbreak of his story hit her, but he was right. He'd fallen apart and she'd paid the price. "You walked away without looking back."

"Everyone hits a wall now and again," he said firmly. "And a kindhearted person gives out second chances because it's the right thing to do. You caught me off guard and I did some stumbling, but then I realized that a man who wants to offer a woman his heart, his home and his life, can't be falling apart over anything."

His heart? Home? Life?

Her heart buzzed.

So did her fingertips.

Mike moved closer. "I'm sorry. I'm sorry I didn't stand tall at that moment, because that's my intention, Carly. To stand strong for you and these kids, and if I have to do it from across the street, I will. But I'd much prefer to have the welcome mat rolled out again. Then if one of us hits a wall, there's backup close by."

She wanted to choose that fairytale option but he'd walked away once. She couldn't bear it if he walked away again.

She shook her head. "I can't, Mike."

He looked deliberately confused. And cute. "Sure you can. It's relatively easy. You say something nice about understanding how I felt, and we move on. I know this is how it's done," he continued, and he aimed that engaging smile her way. "I saw it on TV. And then they say how much they love each other and get married and live happily ever after."

"I don't watch that kind of TV," she told him. "Ever. Happy endings don't just happen. They take hard work and devotion."

"I'm willing to do the work." He moved forward, encroaching on her space a little more. He smelled good and looked better. He reached out one hand to her cheek. "How about you? Can we work together? Because there's nothing in this world I'd like better than to be a part of the family I've grown to love. I figure God brought me to Kendrick Creek for a reason, even if I didn't see it straight off. But maybe I was wrong," he supposed.

Her heart jumped.

"Maybe it was five reasons. Six, if you count the dog."

"Mike, I—"

He kissed her.

He kissed her long and slow and sweet. And someplace between the kiss and the hug that followed, she realized he was right.

Everyone deserved a second chance. Wasn't that the lesson she'd learned as folks passed her around as a child?

He held her tight, his arms looped around her back. She leaned against them and met his gaze. "Kissing is an unfair tactic."

"I consider it advantageous." He smiled and kissed her again. "I want to be part of your life. Forever. And their lives, too. So think about it. Please. We can take it slow."

"I've been going slow for years, Mike. I think I'm ready for the fast lane."

"Yeah?" He leaned back and gave her a lazy smile. A Southern-boy smile that won the heart and soothed the soul. "You won't mind being the sheriff's wife?"

She frowned. "Sheriff?"

"That's why my status was temporary. We were trying each other on, checking the fit. I think I suit the job and it suits me. Now, if the lady in question doesn't mind a husband with a badge…"

"Will you wear your protective vest every single day, no matter what?"

He held up two fingers. "Scout's honor. And I will stand by this family no matter what happens with Gracie. I know what you and Sean are planning," he told her. "I talked with him last night. I also know that things get rough in custody suits but no matter what happens, Carly, I'm here to go the distance. I hope that means I get to go the distance with all four kids, but I'll be here no matter what. If you'll have me."

She reached up for one last, long kiss. "I'll have you, Mike Morris, as long as you're willing to give the kids time to get used to the idea."

"I think a wedding around Thanksgiving would be nice. For all of us. That gives us time before you go back to work. Unless you want to stay home and be with Gracie," he added. "That way we can figure out houses. And stuff. And get to know each other better."

"And youth football season will be over by then," she noted with a wry expression.

His guilty grin said enough. "I wouldn't want a game schedule to take precedence over our wedding, ma'am. That wouldn't be right."

She hugged him. "I know all about Southern boys and their love for football. And I can't think of anything nicer than a Thanksgiving wedding, so yes, Mike Morris. Consider yourself engaged."

He met her smile with his. "I'm going straight to blessed, darlin'. Truly blessed. How about if we take the crew to Dollywood on Saturday to celebrate?"

No fancy dinner out, although she wouldn't mind that now and again. Just the chance to be a family, having fun, building memories. "Perfect, Mike. That would be absolutely perfect."

Epilogue

"Are you sure we have everything ready? Is there anything we've overlooked?" Carly asked Mike on Thanksgiving Day.

"Football, turkey, gravy, corn and smashed taters," he drawled. "We've got it covered, darlin'."

"Dinner's easy," she scolded as he looped his hands around her waist. "It's the wedding I'm thinking about. Have we forgotten anything, Mike?"

"You'll show up at the church as planned?"

"Wearing a pretty dress. Yes."

"And the kids are all involved?"

She frowned. "You know they are. The boys have their suits, and the girls have matching dresses. And shoes. Although that wasn't easy because Hannah doesn't like dresses or fancy shoes, but if she wants to wear pants and a sweatshirt, I don't care because she's doing so well now."

"Sure is."

Hannah was playing on the far side of the living room. She had three dolls set up and was alternately coaching, loving and scolding them in words. Simple words, but words in full sentences.

Gracie was toddling everywhere. There was no keeping her out of Hannah's things, but when Hannah needed a reprieve, she'd take her toys to the bedroom and close the door, and that was way better than wanting to deck her baby sister.

Isaiah was tackling eighth grade with vigor and Isaac thought Mike was great and fifth grade was way too easy.

"We have so much to be thankful for."

"We sure do. And there's this." He handed her a plain white envelope. "From Lida."

Carly's brows drew down, but she tore open the envelope, read the missive and sighed. "She's withdrawing the petition."

"Yes."

"You went to see her?"

He shook his head. "I went to see the social worker and gave her the letter you wrote."

She darted a look toward the upper cupboard.

"Yes. *That* one. When I read it, I knew she had to see it."

"Sean told me not to send it."

Mike made a face. "My brother is stupid smart, but sometimes you've got to meet people where they're at. Your letter was amazing and I thought it would help Lida see things differently. And it did."

"Mike." She reached up and kissed him. "Best wedding gift ever."

He grinned. "She called me yesterday. Said if it would be all right sometime, she'd like to be part of

the kids' lives. Coming to games, to Isaiah's gradua-
tion next spring. That kind of thing. Celebrating their
milestones. But she wasn't sure how you'd feel about it."

"I think that's a good idea as long as she's clean, but
I'd like to talk to them about it first, okay? Sometimes
adults forget that healed wounds can get picked open
and I don't want that for any of the kids."

"Smart and beautiful. And you cook a mean turkey,
because this place smells wonderful. And I might be
starving."

"By the time the boys set the table, I'll have the gravy
made and you can smash those taters you love so well."

He laughed and called the boys to take care of the
table, but when he moved past her to put the drained
potatoes into the big mixing bowl, he leaned close. Real
close. And whispered into her ear, "I do love taters,
ma'am. That's truth. But what I really love is you, Carly
Bradley." He smiled when she blushed. "With all my
heart. And this wedding day can't come soon enough."

"And a two-day honeymoon in Sevierville," she
teased, laughing. "Who needs two weeks in Hawaii
when they've got all this?" She grinned and waved a
hand toward the two boys setting the table and the girls,
not fighting, and playing in the living room.

"Not me," he whispered back. "I've got everything
I need right here. You. Them. And me. God didn't just
put me on the right path last summer, darlin'. He put
me on the best path possible. And here we are. Smash-
ing taters and making gravy with the best of 'em, and
I couldn't ask for anything more."

He was right.

Gracie slept through dinner.

Hannah ate three chicken nuggets and called it a day.

But the rest of them enjoyed an old-fashioned Thanksgiving feast. And when Isaiah declared it was the best Thanksgiving ever, no one disagreed.

Because it was.

* * * * *

If you loved this story,
be sure to pick up the other
Kendrick Creek books

Rebuilding Her Life
The Path Not Taken

And don't miss Ruth Logan Herne's
previous series, Golden Grove

A Hopeful Harvest
Learning to Trust
Finding Her Christmas Family

Available now from Love Inspired!

Find more great reads at
www.LoveInspired.com

Dear Reader,

Life holds some tough twists, doesn't it? We get knocked around and tipped upside down, but we get back up. Dust ourselves off. We keep moving forward because that's what we do.

Life happens. That doesn't make it easy.

Mike and Carly come together from distinctively different backgrounds. Carly's been shuffled around and abandoned throughout her life. She's developed a thick skin and a strong intellect forged by experience. But two surprise children and a new neighbor upset her carefully laid plans.

Mike's been wracked by heartache for over two years. But when he's thrust into the middle of this very special family, threads of peace wrap themselves around his heart and his soul.

Their unlikely relationship has God's timing stamped all over it. It does take these two a little time to see it, and that's true for so many of us, isn't it? Grief and anger can cloud our vision. Faith, hope and love wipe those smudged lenses clean, so I'm wishing each of you a life of faith, hope and love. And the greatest of these is love!

I love hearing from readers. Friend me on Facebook, email me at loganherne@gmail.com and stop by my website ruthloganherne.com. I'd love to get to know you!

Ruthy

**WE HOPE YOU ENJOYED
THIS BOOK FROM**

LOVE INSPIRED

INSPIRATIONAL ROMANCE

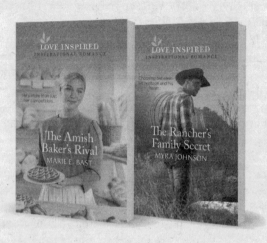

Uplifting stories of faith, forgiveness and hope.

Fall in love with stories where faith helps
guide you through life's challenges, and discover
the promise of a new beginning.

6 NEW BOOKS AVAILABLE EVERY MONTH!

COMING NEXT MONTH FROM
Love Inspired

THE AMISH TWINS NEXT DOOR
Indiana Amish Brides • by Vannetta Chapman

Amish single mom Deborah Mast is determined to raise her seven-year-old twin sons *her* way. But when neighbor Nicholas Stoltzfus takes on the rambunctious boys as apprentices on his farm, she'll learn the value of his help with more than just the children—including how to reopen her heart.

SECRETS IN AN AMISH GARDEN
Amish Seasons • by Lenora Worth

When garden nursery owner Rebecca Eicher hires a new employee, she can't help but notice that Jebediah Martin looks similar to her late fiancé. But when her brother plays matchmaker, Jeb's secret is on the brink of being revealed. Will the truth bring them together or break them apart forever?

EARNING HER TRUST
K-9 Companions • by Brenda Minton

With the help of her service dog, Zeb, Emery Guthrie is finally living a life free from her childhood trauma. Then her high school bully, Beau Wilde, returns to town to care for his best friend's orphaned daughters. Has she healed enough to truly forgive him and let him into her life?

THEIR ALASKAN PAST
Home to Owl Creek • by Belle Calhoune

Opening a dog rescue in Owl Creek, Alaska, is a dream come true for veterinarian Maya Roberts, but the only person she can get to help her run it is her ex-boyfriend Ace Reynolds. When a financial situation forces Ace to accept the position, Maya can't run from her feelings...or the secret of why she ended things.

A NEED TO PROTECT
Widow's Peak Creek • by Susanne Dietze

Dairy shepherdess Clementine Simon's only concern is the safety of her orphaned niece and nephew and *not* the return of her former love Liam Murphy. But could the adventuring globe-trotter be just what she needs to overcome her fears and take another chance on love?

A PROMISE FOR HIS DAUGHTER
by Danielle Thorne

After arriving in Kudzu Creek, contractor and historical preservationist Bradley Ainsworth discovers the two-year-old daughter he never knew about living there with her foster mom, Claire Woodbury. But as they work together updating the house Claire owns, he might find the family he didn't know he was missing...

LOOK FOR THESE AND OTHER LOVE INSPIRED BOOKS WHEREVER BOOKS ARE SOLD, INCLUDING MOST BOOKSTORES, SUPERMARKETS, DISCOUNT STORES AND DRUGSTORES.

LICNM0322

The brick building that housed the county Division of Family Services always brought back a myriad of emotions for Emery Guthrie. As she stood on the sidewalk on a too-warm day in May, the memories came back stronger than ever.

Absently, she reached to pet her service dog, Zeb. The chocolate-brown labradoodle understood that touch and he moved close to her side. He grounded her to reality, to the present. She'd been rescued.

Rescued. She drew on that word. She'd been rescued. By this place, this building and the people inside. They'd seen her father jailed for the abuse that had left her physically and emotionally broken. They'd placed her with a foster mother, Nan Guthrie, the woman who had adopted her as a teen, giving her a new last name and a new life.

But today wasn't about Emery. It was about the two young girls whom Nan had been caring for the past few weeks. They'd lost their parents in a terrible, violent

LIEXP0322

tragedy. They'd been uprooted from their home, their lives and all they'd ever known, brought to Pleasant, Missouri, and placed with Nan until their new guardian could be found.

That man was Beau Wilde. A grade ahead of Emery, Beau had spent their school years making her life even more miserable with his bullying.

He'd taunted, teased and humiliated her.

She shook her head, as if freeing herself from the thoughts she'd not allowed to see the light of day in many years. Those memories belonged in the past.

Just then, a truck pulled off the road and circled the parking lot.

Emery hesitated a moment too long. Beau was out of his truck and heading in her direction. He nodded as he closed in on her.

"Please, let me." He opened the door and stepped back to allow her to go first. "Nice dog."

"Thank you," she whispered. She cleared her throat. "His name is Zeb."

Don't miss
Earning Her Trust *by Brenda Minton*
wherever Love Inspired books and ebooks are sold.

LoveInspired.com

Get 4 FREE REWARDS!

We'll send you 2 FREE Books plus 2 FREE Mystery Gifts.

FREE
Value Over
$20

Both the **Love Inspired** and **Love Inspired** Suspense series feature compelling novels filled with inspirational romance, faith, forgiveness, and hope.

YES! Please send me 2 FREE novels from the Love Inspired or Love Inspired Suspense series and my 2 FREE gifts (gifts are worth about $10 retail). After receiving them, if I don't wish to receive any more books, I can return the shipping statement marked "cancel." If I don't cancel, I will receive 6 brand-new Love Inspired Larger-Print books or Love Inspired Suspense Larger-Print books every month and be billed just $5.99 each in the U.S. or $6.24 each in Canada. That is a savings of at least 17% off the cover price. It's quite a bargain! Shipping and handling is just 50¢ per book in the U.S. and $1.25 per book in Canada.* I understand that accepting the 2 free books and gifts places me under no obligation to buy anything. I can always return a shipment and cancel at any time. The free books and gifts are mine to keep no matter what I decide.

Choose one: ☐ **Love Inspired**
Larger-Print
(122/322 IDN GNWC)

☐ **Love Inspired Suspense**
Larger-Print
(107/307 IDN GNWN)

Name (please print)

Address   Apt. #

City   State/Province   Zip/Postal Code

Email: Please check this box ☐ if you would like to receive newsletters and promotional emails from Harlequin Enterprises ULC and its affiliates. You can unsubscribe anytime.

Mail to the Harlequin Reader Service:
IN U.S.A.: P.O. Box 1341, Buffalo, NY 14240-8531
IN CANADA: P.O. Box 603, Fort Erie, Ontario L2A 5X3

Want to try 2 free books from another series? Call 1-800-873-8635 or visit www.ReaderService.com.

*Terms and prices subject to change without notice. Prices do not include sales taxes, which will be charged (if applicable) based on your state or country of residence. Canadian residents will be charged applicable taxes. Offer not valid in Quebec. This offer is limited to one order per household. Books received may not be as shown. Not valid for current subscribers to the Love Inspired or Love Inspired Suspense series. All orders subject to approval. Credit or debit balances in a customer's account(s) may be offset by any other outstanding balance owed by or to the customer. Please allow 4 to 6 weeks for delivery. Offer available while quantities last.

Your Privacy—Your information is being collected by Harlequin Enterprises ULC, operating as Harlequin Reader Service. For a complete summary of the information we collect, how we use this information and to whom it is disclosed, please visit our privacy notice located at corporate.harlequin.com/privacy-notice. From time to time we may also exchange your personal information with reputable third parties. If you wish to opt out of this sharing of your personal information, please visit readerservice.com/consumerschoice or call 1-800-873-8635. **Notice to California Residents**—Under California law, you have specific rights to control and access your data. For more information on these rights and how to exercise them, visit corporate.harlequin.com/california-privacy.

LIRLIS22

IF YOU ENJOYED THIS BOOK, DON'T MISS NEW EXTENDED-LENGTH NOVELS FROM LOVE INSPIRED!

In addition to the Love Inspired books you know and love, we're excited to introduce even more uplifting stories in a longer format, with more inspiring fresh starts and page-turning thrills!

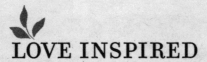

LOVE INSPIRED

Stories to uplift and inspire.

Fall in love with Love Inspired—inspirational and uplifting stories of faith and hope. Find strength and comfort in the bonds of friendship and community. Revel in the warmth of possibility, and the promise of new beginnings.

LOOK FOR THESE LOVE INSPIRED TITLES ONLINE AND IN THE BOOK DEPARTMENT OF YOUR FAVORITE RETAILER!